THE FEAST

Books by Kathryn Elizabeth Jones

A River of Stones

Parable Series

    Conquering Your Goliaths: A Parable of the Five Stones

    Conquering Your Goliaths: Guidebook

    The Feast: A Parable of the Ring

    The Gift: A Parable of the Key

    The Parables of Virginia Bean

Heaven 24/7 - Living in the Light

Marketing Your Book on a Budget

Susan Cramer Mysteries

    Scrambled

    Sunny Side-Up

    Hard Boiled

    Over Easy

Brianne James Mysteries

    Tie Died

    Buckled Inn

The Space Adventures of Aaden Prescott

    Light*Shade*

    Light*Descending* – Spring 2019

    Light*Source* – Fall 2020

Mooseberry Mooseberry Gooseberry Pie

THE FEAST

A Parable of the Ring

Book II

KATHRYN ELIZABETH JONES

Idea Creations Press
www.ideacreationspress.com

Idea Creations Press
www.ideacreationspress.com

Copyright © Kathryn Elizabeth Jones, 2013.

This is a work of fiction. Any resemblance of
characters to actual persons, living or dead, is purely
coincidental.

ISBN-13: 978-0-9888107-2-3

ACKNOWLEDGMENT

To my husband: The bearer of many gifts including the nudge that this book needed to be written.

Preface

In *Conquering Your Goliaths: A Parable of the Five Stones*, Ms. Virginia Bean meets God and through the five stones: **Listening, Trust, Optimism, Tenacity** and **Constancy**, she learns a few things. About herself. About her relationship with God. About her relationship with others.

Listening teaches Virginia how to keep still long enough to listen to God.

She Learns to **trust** in God always, even if she doesn't agree.

Optimism keeps her thinking positive no matter what she faces.

And **Tenacity** plays a big factor in moving her forward despite the obstacles.

Constancy, well, let's just say that it teaches her the importance of walking with God always. In good times and in bad.

Consider that even in the best of circumstances and the most difficult of trials, a person has a way of drifting away from the source of all happiness.

The Feast – A Parable of the Ring

Like now, for example.

The End

Her marriage with Richard was over. This was something Virginia knew for sure. She also knew she must have imagined the stones' supreme power and her awakening with God.

As she sat on the couch that still sported a hole large enough for a rock to pass through, she smiled at it sadly, touched the worn fibers of the cloth filling it's gap and thought of Richard and how much she missed him. She thought of her life, alone again, without a husband, without a child.

They'd been married five years and during that time Virginia had used the stones and what they represented in her life with Richard. He'd agreed that they held a power, and they'd displayed them on the mantel for all to see.

Except the stones hadn't given them a child, and after three years of relentless doctor visits, tests and more tests, Virginia was tired of it all and Richard was gone.

He said he loved her. She said she loved him, but without a child their marriage seemed a void, a mistake. She thought of Richard, imagined him alone in a hotel room outside of town. It was winter and the air was bitter, icy and dry to her skin. Her skin felt like sandpaper and her throat practically closed off at night as she breathed in the stagnant air.

Just like her life.

Virginia walked to the bedroom and to her side of the bed. A tear dropped onto her pillow. The side next to hers still held Richard's pillow. She reached for it and pushed it against her chest, breathing in the scent of him, sort of an Irish Spring with a smattering of spruce.

It was the trees he loved best, and they'd spent many days following their wedding hiking the mountains and sitting next to plants and communicating with them.

It didn't seem so natural now, but then, right after she'd discovered it, it was like the power of the stones enveloped everything and everyone she knew. At the wedding, long lost friends and family who never dreamed she'd wed, and even the flowers and other natural growth near the lake, breathed in their love and she could feel their presence.

She knew God was there. She'd felt him too. In the days following her wedding she hoped he'd come to her again or direct her to meet with him, but he never did. The stones sat on the mantel, and although she was reminded of their glow or colors from time to time, life caught up with her and her business began growing faster than she could keep up with it.

Just Desserts. Using Richard's place, a log cabin built only 10 minutes from the city, she'd grown her business both in clientele and opportunity. Many people taking her awakening courses had found their lives improved and their own businesses and personal life, soaring.

But the fights and lonely nights without Richard had finally taken its toll. He hadn't returned and it had been a week.

She dared not teach, for in teaching she would see him. And so she'd cancelled her classes and hired a runner to take what she had baked from home to Richard's place on the corner of *North Shore* and *Main*. Though she'd done plenty of baking there since meeting Richard, now it just seemed awkward.

What would she do now?

She stood and reached for the white stone but as she stood there, feeling the veins in the rock's surface, it didn't speak to her. She wanted to hold the black rock, but hesitated. No, she'd leave it there. She wouldn't reach for the other rocks, she couldn't.

All was lost.

The Ring

Richard had never loved a woman as much as he loved Virginia, her weirdness included. He'd accepted the five stones, had lived with her desires to be perfect, had even helped her work through the pains of her doubting heart, but the one thing that they lacked together had reached forth its tentacles and pierced his soul as well as hers.

Why wouldn't God allow them to have a child?

The doughnuts had arrived again in perfect order, though he knew that his wife was faring much worse. Her classes cancelled, folks coming to the bakery had dwindled until even the bakery sales hadn't given them a reason to return.

He couldn't reach her. Heck, he couldn't reach himself. God had brought them together, he knew that. As he stood in the center of the room where he'd first gotten a glimpse of her, the stirring returned. Tears welled in his eyes as he thought of her standing by the window. He could almost see her, could almost hear the doves in the distance, but the windows were iced over and the room felt too heated, too dark.

He turned when he heard the bell.

An old man stood before him.

"What would you like today, Sir?" he asked.

The old man shifted his shoulders. He wore a black and white checkered shirt, corduroy pants the color of wet dirt and a fishing cap.

"My wi...I mean these doughnuts are terrific," Richard said when the man said nothing.

"What makes them terrific?" The man leaned closer to the counter and took a deep sniff. "It's hard to smell them through the glass."

Richard tried not to smirk. The man must be deranged or something.

"Do you like chocolate?"

The old man touched his white beard. "I like chocolate."

The man was silent for some time and it seemed to Richard that he was looking at each doughnut individually, sort of examining each one with his eyes. Virginia had not only made chocolate but chocolate with sprinkles and the heavy duty filled kind. Today there was raspberry, lemon and meringue.

"What do you think of the colors?" the old man asked. "Does the color of the doughnut make it taste better?"

Richard thought the question odd. It was like asking if a brown doughnut was better than a pink, frosted one. "Do you have a favorite color?" he asked.

"I like all colors," said the man.

Richard wondered if the old man was just speaking about doughnuts. Just then a young girl came up to the counter. "I want a cupcake," she said.

The old man smiled. "You'd better get her that cupcake. I can wait."

Richard walked over to help the young girl. She was a tiny thing, probably only five or six. "Where's your mother?" he asked first.

"Down that way." The girl pointed in the direction of the dairy department.

"Would you rather have a doughnut?" he asked. Virginia hadn't delivered any cupcakes today and he was out.

The girl peered inside the glass. "The pink one with the diamond in it," she said.

Richard smiled, he couldn't help it. The young girl had cheered him up. Unfortunately, there wasn't a cupcake with a diamond in it.

"I'm sorry..." he began, but the girl was pointing. "There, in the corner."

Sure enough, when Richard looked to the corner of the case he could see something glittering a-top a bright pink cupcake. He reached inside the case and pulled it out. The ring was fake but it still glittered against the countertop glass.

"That's it!" squealed the girl, reaching for the bobble. She took the cupcake from his hands. He could see her pulling the ring from the pink frosting and licking it off. He thought of pink, the typical favorite color for a girl, and watched the young girl until she was out of sight. Hopefully with her mother, he thought. But when he turned to help the old man he was no longer there.

Richard thought more about the pink cupcake with the ring on it that night at the hotel. He wondered where it had come from and hoped the little girl had been safe in eating the cupcake. He decided to call Virginia.

"So, you say that I must have made some pink cupcakes?" she asked.

Richard nodded, though his wife couldn't see the gesture. "Yes," he added wearily into the phone. "You must have made some, I'm just having a difficult time remembering."

"But I haven't made cupcakes for at least...oh, two months or so. They sell better when it's warm out. Are you taking in a new vendor?"

Richard didn't even have to think about that one. He hadn't had a new vendor since she'd joined him five years ago; hadn't a need of a vendor. Her stuff was great.

"No new vendor. It's funny, you know. This old man came up to the counter. Pretty strange, if you ask me, and then there was this little girl pointing to a pink cupcake with a ring in it."

"Did you say a ring?" Virginia asked.

"Yes. It was right there on top of the pink cupcake, glittering away. The ring was fake, of course."

"Of course. So where do you think it came from?"

Richard had no idea. It suddenly occurred to him that they were speaking for the first time in a week; actually speaking, not yelling or blaming the other person. It was nice. "So, when will you be returning back to work?" he asked.

There was sudden silence on the other end. "I don't know. Maybe when I'm feeling a bit better."

"Are you sick?"

"Of course not, especially in the way you might be thinking," she countered.

Her voice sounded strange, almost foreign to him; so it was going to end the same way. "Take your time," he said.

"I'll do that."

There was a sudden emptiness on the other end of the line and Richard knew that she'd hung up.

That night Richard dreamt of the ring. It floated above him like a glittering specter. He saw it again atop the pink cupcake as the girl licked the pink frosting off the ring on her forefinger.

***

Virginia tossed and turned. Why had Richard called her for such a stupid reason? A pink cupcake? It just didn't make sense. She got up, and although it was near 3 a.m., started on a batch of cupcakes. If this was his way of getting more work out of her, well, she'd do it. She couldn't sleep anyway and thoughts of creating strawberry cupcakes with pink frosting and a sweet ring on top did something to her; something she just couldn't put her finger on.

She laughed at her own joke and got busy. In time, the smell of strawberry jam filled the space in her kitchen and all she could think about was getting her hands on those fake rings that Richard had spoken about.

She knew of a craft store nearby that might have them, and as the batter swirled and became a luscious pink, she thought of him.

Richard had won her over early on. But it had never been about the ring. It had been more about the heart. He'd only been able to afford a small diamond; she looked at it now on her third finger and smiled. The band was silver, and a small, white stone was tucked into its center like a warm blanket. It had been enough.

He understood her and had loved the way she loved life. The hikes were magnificent; almost as if she was reaching God by hiking to the mountain's peek... A sudden thought came to her mind of a tall tower reaching to the heavens but she shrugged it off. It was just like her to ruin a good thought with a bad one.

The cupcake papers ready, Virginia poured the mixture inside, making sure to leave enough space for rising. She laughed at herself again, remembering the cupcakes she'd first made with her mother, now gone. She recalled how her mother had scolded her for filling the cups too full. She'd made her scoop up the goop on the pan and reuse it in other cups. And then she thought of Paul and God. For it was Paul who'd persuaded her to begin *Just Desserts* in the first place and it was God who'd kept her going.

And now?

She remembered the first time the stones had sat still without working and how alone she'd felt. She was frustrated, yes, about the baby she would never have, but she'd felt assured that God would help her. Hadn't he always?

She placed the pan in the heated oven and sat down on one of her kitchen chairs. The legs scraped momentarily against the hardwood floor as she pulled the chair to the table. With nothing before her but her memories, she placed her hands on her head and cried.

It had been just yesterday since she'd spilled a tear and now it came in a rushing stream. It just wasn't fair, none of it! She was alone, again! And God had done nothing to help her!

The sobbing was followed by an embarrassing runny nose. She stood and walked to the bathroom, grabbed a tissue and returned to the kitchen. Just 10 minutes left.

***

Richard got up from the hotel bed and took a shower. He briefly thought of the stones, but shrugged the thought aside. They'd worked for Virginia for a while, so long that she had grown so accustomed to their help that something had happened to her; a drifting of sorts had occurred. It was a natural drifting, he thought. Sort of like she figured the help of God should come to her without her having to work for it.

He'd called it a stronger focus on change, a step-up, and Virginia had yelled at him. "What do you think, that I'm a loser or something?" she'd shouted. As if not getting pregnant was suddenly her fault when they'd discovered months before that it was his.

They'd spoken of adoption, but Virginia had wanted her own child. And she'd said it like having a baby finally made things perfect for her; having a child of her own.

Richard just didn't get it. Wasn't it bad enough that it was his fault and that she'd probably married the

19

wrong man? He could hardly live with himself knowing that he was the cause of her unhappiness, and it was no wonder that she couldn't live with him either.

He stepped out of the shower, toweled off and got dressed, still thinking of the woman he'd fallen in love with. He wished they'd never spoken about having children.

***

By 5 a.m. the cupcakes were finished and Virginia was exhausted. She loaded the cupcakes into the cardboard carrier, wrapping the plastic loosely over the top, and carried the carriers one at a time to the car. No, she still didn't have a van – that one had been next on the agenda before Richard left her. But Paul's old car, which still looked as new as the day it was driven off the lot, would work. She'd promised him that she'd take care of it and she had. She had the detailing done on the car once a month and kept the outside to a spit shine. He would have been proud.

She was a few minutes early but had a key to the bakery area. Once inside, Virginia avoided the secret room (although she had to walk through it to get to the counter), and placed the cupcakes on the other side of the glass. The rings weren't on the cupcakes yet, but that didn't matter. As soon as the craft store opened she'd run over, pick up what she needed, and add the last bit of decor to the fluffy pink tops.

As it was, she'd have to deal with her husband. Much better to get the cupcakes shelved than have him offer to carry them for her. Once in place, Virginia looked around. There were a few food stockers in the small, country store, but no one else. Boxes filled the few aisles as they were opened and their treasures deposited on various shelves.

Shutting the glass counter door, she turned, made her way back through the secret room where she'd held many classes and shared her thoughts about growth and the power of God. But when she reached the door she was not alone.

She wanted it to be God with everything that was in her; wanted him to see her, embrace her. It was so unlike her to be dreaming about something that hadn't occurred in years but yet that's what she was doing; thinking of him in those awful corduroy pants and tattered fisherman's hat. Tears were suddenly welling as Richard opened the door.

"So, you've decided to show up," he said. It appeared that he was embarrassed, but he didn't recall his words. Instead he added, "I can use all the help I can get. Baking today?"

Virginia shook her head. "Not today. I've got some cupcakes in the cabinet. Just heading to the craft store." She noticed that his hair wasn't brushed, and that his blue eyes appeared clouded over. He was suffering.

For a moment she stopped but no words came. She felt the warmth of the room and the way her skin tingled at the thought of him touching her. But she couldn't speak.

"Cupcakes. What kind?" he asked.

"Pink ones just like you wanted. I just need to go and get the rings."

Richard appeared to consider her words. He directed her to the window. "Have you noticed how icy the glass is?" he asked.

She nodded. "Nothing like summer."

"But look how beautiful it is. See that long icicle?"

There was a large one that reached from the top of the room, well past the window, and almost to the snow below.

"I know things are tough, but I think it's going to be okay."

"What do you mean, okay? I want my life to be better than okay."

She felt the smell of spruce next to her, like Christmas that was still there, but he didn't touch her. "I'm sorry," he said.

"So am I."

"Since that little girl asked for that pink cupcake, I've been thinking a lot about you."

"You're kidding." It seemed funny that her husband would associate a pink cupcake with anything having to do with her.

"You know, that old man with the fisherman's cap and old corduroys scared me a little, I think."

"What old man?"

"The one at the counter."

She touched the glass with her forefinger thinking of the ring. Perhaps all hope wasn't lost after all. He was going to apologize now, tell her it was all his fault, ask her to forgive him.

"The old man. You know, he sort of reminds me of the old guy that came to the counter years ago and handed me that constancy stone that you no longer use."

She was angry. How dare he... and then she noticed that her heart was racing. An old man who looked like God? Impossible.

"You sure it was him?"

"I didn't say that."

She turned. His blue eyes had cleared and he was looking deeply into her own. She thought she saw love there. "So?"

"I said that he reminded me of him."

"So, what did the old guy look like? What was he wearing?"

"He had a beard, a checkered shirt, some old pants, a fisherman's cap, like I said, why?"

"You're kidding." Her heart stopped and, in its place, a small light began to glow. "Are you sure?"

"I'm sure about what he was wearing."

"But what if it was God? Did you feel anything different when he was there? Did you notice anything, anything at all?"

Richard shrugged his shoulders. "Not really. Well, except..."

"Except what?" The glow she'd felt in her heart had suddenly changed to something akin to excitement.

"That pink cupcake with the ring on it appeared seconds after he arrived."

The Feast – A Parable of the Ring

The Vow

After a quick trip to the craft store, Virginia returned with the rings. She placed each glittering stone atop a single cupcake. Once finished she looked over at Richard.

"What do you think it means?" he asked.

"I have no idea," she answered, but her heart was still pumping with excitement. After all this, all these years, she'd finally be able to speak to him again. And then a new thought occurred to her. "So, why do you think he came to you first?"

Richard shrugged. The store had just opened and he was busily putting the new batch of cookies into the case. "Maybe I was at the right place at the right time."

"What's that supposed to mean?"

"Just what I said. I was here, he came – if it was him." He turned from her and went to the cooling counter.

She considered his words. It was God and she was going to reach him if it was the last thing she did.

There was that tower again to heaven. She looked back at Richard. He was gathering another sheet of cookies.

"Really, Virginia, I'm here all of the time serving customers."

"While I'm at home feeling sorry for myself, is that it?"

"Now you're putting words in my mouth." He slid the second batch of cookies inside and turned to her, placing his hand on her shoulder. She flinched.

"Sorry. Maybe you're just making a mountain out of a molehill. Maybe it was just some old guy."

"It was God," said Virginia.

And so she decided to stay and work with her husband the entire day. They sold doughnuts, a few pink cupcakes and plenty of cookies, but God didn't show up and Virginia went home miserable. Still, she wasn't alone.

In the car Richard spoke about getting the classes started up again. But she couldn't do that. He inferred that it would help her. That it would probably assist her in connecting again with God. "When was the last time you prayed?" he'd asked, before she'd become angry and threatened to leave him for good.

He knew she hadn't prayed ever since the final results had come in. She hadn't prayed because she was too angry to pray. She hadn't prayed, because God knew how she was feeling. Why wouldn't he just step in and fix it? No, she hadn't prayed, and she wouldn't be praying now.

***

26

Richard snuggled on the old couch as best as he could, trying to avoid the hole. Amazing, really, how they'd kept the couch with the defect for so many years, but it was comforting to him, somehow. Virginia had told him all about the stone of trust, how it had burned through the fabric and to the floor, and Richard wondered if that was what was happening now. Trust, or lack of it.

He wondered if he was partially to blame. Sure, he believed his wife, but she put so much stock in the stones that it had been difficult, if not impossible, for her to think about anything else. It was like she was waking and sleeping stones, and it was unlike him not to believe her, he just didn't get it – at least not all of it.

And then the business had grown and things had changed for his wife. She no longer held the stones. Some days she didn't even look at them. And then came the day she no longer spoke about them; it seemed to him that it was just easier for her to get up, shower and go about the day than to think about them.

Richard wondered if that had caused it, or if he was only imagining the change occurring then and not when they found out that they couldn't have a baby. They'd completed the nursery, had purchased clothing that could be used for either a boy or a girl, had purchased a crib and all that goes with it, painted the room an *either way* yellow, but nothing had happened. Virginia had been sure about that, just as she was sure about most things in their marriage. *If we buy the right stuff, then the baby will be conceived. If we do all the testing required, the baby will come.* But the baby hadn't come.

The Feast – A Parable of the Ring

The night was a long one as Richard slept on the couch, his home away from home without having to go to the hotel. Well, at least he was making progress.

***

Virginia was questioning everything and it didn't matter that her husband had already picked up his things at the hotel and had made his way to work. She knew this because a matted lump of blankets caressed the couch and floor and dirty socks, shirts and pants lay near the hamper – though not directly in it.

If God had reached out to her husband, and she had no doubt that he had, why him and not her? What was she doing wrong? She'd long since wondered if God had merely forgotten about her; he had millions of children after all. Perhaps what she needed was a swift kick on the backside, but her heart still ached for the companionship she'd once had.

The door to the nursery was open just a crack. Either she'd forgotten to shut it or her husband had been there just that morning. It was 6 a.m. and he was already at work; the man was quick in the morning, but sloppy in the process.

The glow of the sun coming through the window made her think of God, if only for a moment, and then she was folding and refolding the blankets, straightening the little diapers and nightshirts, and winding her way to a small bookshelf that housed all of her favorite children's books. She sat in the wooden rocker and opened the first book her hands reached but it didn't take long for her eyes to cloud with tears. In only moments she couldn't see the words, but she could feel in her heart the emptiness of the child that would never be hers.

It wasn't fair!

Tears formed in her throat. She couldn't breathe. The sun, its rays piercing the thin draperies, filtered to her eyes and made her blink. But even then, she didn't hear him, she didn't hear him.

This was her daily routine after Richard went to work, and it was just easier for him not to know. She didn't blame him, not really, she just ached so much for a child. It was like she was missing a part of herself. The book sat opened, and as Virginia rocked in the chair that held no child, she wrapped the small yellow blanket around herself. It was warm, and in moments she imagined her child was there.

***

The old man stood in front of him, his long beard as full as he last remembered it, the same checkered shirt and old brown corduroys reminding him of a muddy lake in April just before the thaw. And he had on that old hat as if he was just stopping by before doing some fishing.

"So, I see your wife made some pink cupcakes," he said.

Richard's heart was already pounding. If Virginia was right he was talking with God and it was one thing to talk with him when you didn't know it and quite another to speak with him when you did. He felt his legs growing soft and the tips of his fingers tingling.

"I... ah...yes, my wife."

"They look nice," the old man said, looking down. "Only, the rings, they don't quite glitter as much as the one you had in the case the other day. "

Richard looked into the case. God was right. They were all rings with a fake diamond like before, but the rings didn't glisten this time.

"Well, they're pretty cheap," he said. "The one that was in the case the day before yesterday may have cost you more."

"Me?" asked the gentleman, touching his beard.

"You...did bring the cupcake with the ring on it yesterday," stumbled Richard.

"Why would you think that?" The old gent stopped looking at the cupcakes and his blue eyes warmed Richard's. Perhaps...this was God.

"I just know...the child...ah...I didn't have that cupcake in the case until...after you arrived."

"Well, I'll be," said God. "You are correct."

"I am?" stammered Richard. "I mean, why would you bring me a pink cupcake with a fake ring in it?"

The old man smiled. "Well, if I told you that, that would take away some searching on your part, wouldn't it?"

"I imagine so." He suddenly knew that God could read his mind, and if he was reading it in this very moment God had to know how petrified he was.

"But I'll give you a clue," said God. "I like giving clues when my child is especially afraid. That way, you don't have to faint and you don't have to feel as if you're losing your stomach."

Richard nodded.

"The diamond was real."

It took a few moments for the comment to register. "You mean, that little girl got a real diamond ring? She didn't even pay for the cupcake!"

"That's right," said God. "She didn't pay, but her family needed it or, you could say, the money that was needed that only that cupcake could deliver, was offered."

Richard couldn't believe it. And yet, God was standing right there telling him that it was true. "So, my wife didn't really need to make all of those pink cupcakes then?"

"What do you think?"

Richard blinked. What did he think? Was this really God? Had he provided the pink cupcake with the ring on top to teach him something? And if so, what?

"I think I need to talk with my wife about this." Richard looked away for only a moment. He imagined the young girl leaving him, the ring on her forefinger, her tiny fingers wet with pink frosting. But he shouldn't have looked away.

Looking back the man was gone.

In that moment he wanted to call Virginia on his cell phone, but that didn't feel like the right way to talk about a communication with God so Richard waited the entire day to tell his wife what had happened. When she didn't show up for work in the afternoon he wanted to close up shop but knew that he couldn't, and when the evening arrived and she was still not there, he took a few deep breaths and anxiously awaited their time together at home.

For moral support or for use in his imminent object lesson of sorts, he brought along one of her pink cupcakes. It sat next to him in a small box.

***

"You what?" Virginia shrieked. She couldn't believe it. God had come to him again! Again! "So, what did he say this time?" she asked irritably. A distinct impression came to her mind that she'd been through this one before. It was sort of like explaining the power of the five stones to her friend, Paul, all over again. He hadn't believed her at first, and she was having a hard time believing her husband.

"He admitted to bringing the first pink cupcake."

"The one you gave to the girl."

"He said the diamond was real."

"What?"

"The ring that I gave to that girl. The ring, it was real."

"Virginia was silent."

"It was hard enough that I knew I was talking to God, and then he told me that the little girl got that cupcake with the diamond ring in it because the money was needed for her family."

"Unbelievable! said Virginia.

"Believe it," said Richard. "So, what do you think it means?"

Virginia couldn't do anything but shrug. "Well, how should I know?" she finally said. "I mean, God isn't speaking to me anymore. He obviously prefers you." She hesitated. "You must be doing something right."

"Just listening," said Richard.

"Don't throw that one in my face." Virginia felt her face grow hot. She shouldn't have said it, but it was exactly how she felt. She placed her hands on her head, and just like the morning she'd made the pink cupcakes, she began to cry. Small tears fell at first and then the sobs arrived in all their glory. Before she knew it, Richard had reached for her and was holding her close.

Later, he withdrew the pink cupcake with the fake diamond setting on top and they talked for hours about its possible meaning. Rings sometimes meant friendship, but a diamond ring usually meant marriage. In the case of the little girl, however, it must have meant 'means' – having the means to provide.

The next morning Virginia cooked her husband breakfast. It was 5 a.m. but she felt that she needed to do this. The night before he'd been tremendously supportive. She must have cried 2 hours – at least. It was his favorite: scrambled eggs, bacon and pancakes. She was just finishing up the last dollop when he walked in.

"I knew something good was in here," he said, looking at the feast and kissing her neck. She wasn't sure if he meant the breakfast or herself. It made her happy and tingly.

"The juice is already on the table."

He sat and poured a glass. "Do you know," he said, "we haven't had breakfast together since I can't remember when."

But she remembered, though she didn't want to bring it up. "Do you think we should take the nursery down?" she asked.

He chewed for a moment. "I don't know. I kind of like it." She didn't want to tell him that she had spent every morning for months in that room, rocking with no one, reading to no one, but she just wasn't ready to tell him her secret.

"I like the room, too." She dished up her plate and sat across from him at the table. It was especially cold out this morning and so she'd worn her old robe and slippers. He already had his working duds on; cream colored pants and a navy button up shirt. His hair was combed like she liked it and he wore a smile larger than she'd seen in months.

"This is good," he finally said. His plate was almost empty. She'd taken two bites.

"Would you like some more?"

"Pancakes if you have them." She felt suddenly as if they were in a restaurant, but after five years of marriage she knew Richard's ways. He was thoughtful, serious for the most part, and used proper etiquette when the occasion warranted.

She got up and reached for the pancake plate. He took his fork and stabbed the first two gems from the stack. "Have you thought any more about the meaning of the ring?" she asked.

He chewed, swallowed and then said, "I have, and I'm wondering if we're right in both cases. In the first case we have a young girl with a poor family. She gets a cupcake with a ring. When her mother discovers the prize, she realizes the ring can be sold and the money provided. In the second case, the ring is for us.

We made some pretty heavy-duty commitments to each other the day we became husband and wife." He paused, and Virginia wasn't sure if he paused for effect or for something else.

"An all-knowing God might just teach two things at one time," he added.

It was an interesting thought. Give the little girl the money she needed; remind them of the commitments they'd made to each other – the ring, a symbol of that commitment. "It feels right," said Virginia, "but how can we be sure?"

"I prayed about it last night," said Richard.

"You what?"

"Prayed. And I think it worked. I think God is trying to tell us something."

***

Virginia wasn't going to miss out on seeing God ever again. She traveled to work with her husband the entire next week and the week following, and though sales began to increase, the old man in the corduroys had not made an appearance. In addition, she still hadn't begun her classes and by the third week she just couldn't go back. Richard was disappointed. He told her not to worry and to let God take care of it, which only made her angry enough to stomp out of the hidden room and to her car.

Once home she cloistered herself inside the nursery, though it was noon, and read and rocked the child that wasn't there. This time, however, the experience was hurtful. It didn't feel the same. It was all fake, this preparing for a baby that would never come. She couldn't do it anymore.

Anger coursed through her. She reached for the thin draperies and tugged them from the window. She attacked the walls next, breaking the lamp and small end tables in the process. As the heat erupted within her, she took apart the crib, bit by bit until all that was left was spindles, box springs and side pieces. These she shoved out the nursery window. They clanked against the house and fell to the icy snow beneath. She didn't even look out the window to see how they'd landed. She didn't care.

Turning from the window, Virginia reached inside the closet and pulled out the little outfits from their hangers. Sobbing, she tossed them out the window. They fluttered and were gone. She attacked the dresser and the changing table next, withdrawing anything inside and tossing the contents out the window with the other things. The books were last.

As she held the last treasure in her hands, a book her own mother had read to her as a child, she tore the pages one by one from the book's spine. This was the hardest feat of all. It was as if she was telling God that not even the relationship with her mother mattered.

As the tears fell, she watched each piece coast to the floor like a paper bird. Now she was finished. She could go on and she didn't care if God ever spoke to her again.

Virginia slammed the door.

***

Kathryn Elizabeth Jones

Richard was beyond angry. He looked at the disheveled nursery and thought about his wife already asleep in their bed. He'd known something was wrong the moment he'd driven up. Not only were the baby's things all over the snow, but most were broken or torn.

He left the nursery and entered the bedroom. Whether his wife was faking sleep or not it did not matter. It was time to talk.

***

"I don't care!"

"But I do!"

Virginia wrapped the pillow around her face and tried to go back to sleep. It was late and she was tired but he wouldn't stop bothering her. She'd probably reacted without thinking, she knew that now, and Richard was going to tell her what she knew already.

"Virginia." The words were soft and she almost missed them under her pillow. But they were there. "Honey. We need to talk."

"Why?" she mumbled behind the barrier. "Why?"

"I know you feel bad about the baby."

"Bad doesn't even touch it. I'm miserable."

"Remove the pillow so we can talk. Okay, honey?"

From the corner of the pillow she peeked out. Large tears were running down her husband's cheeks. And he wasn't wiping them off.

"I love you, you silly," he said, removing the rest of the pillow from her face. "Don't you know that?"

"I just can't believe," she sniffed, "that we're not going to have a baby."

"I know, I know." Richard caressed her hair. Before she knew it, he was lying beside her and holding her close. The feeling was nice.

"Don't hate...me," she wheezed. "I did a... stupid thing."

"It wasn't stupid. You were angry, that's all."

"Angry enough to wreck everything in that room."

"We can clean it up."

She wondered where the lecture was but it didn't come. Instead, Richard lay by her. He continued to stroke her hair. "We will get through this."

"IIow?"

"With God's help."

"But how do you know he'll help us? I mean, he won't talk to me and he'll only talk to you when I'm not there."

Richard wiped away another tear from her face.

"Why do you think that is?" he asked.

"I don't know, because I'm a grump." She sniffed again. "I'm angry at him. He has full control over giving us a child, but somehow he doesn't think we deserve it."

Richard remained silent. For a time Virginia wondered if he'd fallen asleep. And then he said, "I don't think it has anything to do with deserving something. Did you deserve to be single all of those years? And your friend, Paul, did he deserve to die?"

"Of course not."

"Then why would you think that you don't deserve to have a child. Remember it's my fault. I am the one that can't get you pregnant. You should be angry with me."

"But I am angry at you!"

There was a slight loosening of the hug, but Richard didn't move away.

She continued, "I mean, all this time. I was single for so long and when I found you I thought, well, now I can finally get my life started! I'm married to a man I love and now it's time to have children."

"Is that the only reason you married me? For children?"

"Of course not. I...I just want children, that's all." She was wetting the pillowcase with her runny nose but she didn't care.

"What if we're not supposed to have children? What if God has another answer for us?"

Virginia thought about that. Nothing could be better than bringing children into the world and if she couldn't have any of her own, what was the point?

"You remember our vows." His voice was quiet, almost as if he was struggling to keep his tone in check. "I remember that we promised to love one another through sickness and health and for better or for worse. If we never have a child would it really be such a bad thing?"

Virginia's tears had dried. She wiped her nose with her shirt sleeve and thought about her husband's words. She remembered that moment at the altar and what she'd promised him. Still, it didn't make things any easier. She wanted a child and there was no way that she could see to work her way around that feeling...

***

"Richard!" Richard sat bolt upright. His blond hair had taken a beating from the night before; it went every which way, and he was still wearing his clothes and shoes.

She laughed. She couldn't help it.

"What?" he bumbled. "What?"

"You slept in your clothes. You never do that."

He laughed back, licked his hand, and tried to flatten his hair.

"You never do that either," said Virginia.

"Well, maybe it's about time that I did. I'm sorry. You needed someone and I just didn't know how to be there for you."

She thought about the night before and wondered what he could mean. He'd done all of the right things, but then again, she'd finally been ready to receive them. To receive. Her mind caught hold upon a thought, a reoccurring thought that had never really left her. The tower. It was always about building the tower to God or climbing the mountain, or something.

She sat. "You need to get to work."

"I know, I just wanted to make sure you were alright. Are you coming today?" He stood and walked to the bathroom, tugging at and dropping his clothing and shoes as he went. She heard the faucet turn on.

Was she going to work with her husband? Of course she was. How could she go anywhere else?

***

Richard stood by the bakery shelves. There had been a call for chocolate the last few days and Richard had said nothing to Virginia about it. But now, somehow, he felt it would be okay.

"Do we need cookies, or what?" she asked.

"Chocolate. Can you go to Wholesale Max's? I probably shouldn't leave."

With their late arrival had come a fair share of strange looks and a few put out customers. Richard had tried to make it up to them with a free cookie but this had caused even more emptiness within the shelves.

"Sure," she said. "I'll be back soon."

Virginia went through the secret doors as usual, but this time, she thought seriously about getting her classes started again. After work she'd clean up the mess she'd made at home and then make some calls. Previous students might be interested in a new class, and even if they weren't they might know of someone who was.

In the car, Virginia traveled north. It took about 15 minutes to get to Wholesale Max's. She picked up the chocolate, packaged in bulk, and had almost reached the door when she saw him. Unbelievably he was at the magazine stand, and if she hadn't looked in his direction at exactly the right time she might have missed him.

He was the same as she remembered him. Brown corduroys, a flannel shirt, white beard...

His eyes turned in her direction and he smiled. It was like the sun had come out in just that moment.

She walked toward him, bag in hand. "So, what are you doing here?" she asked.

"Just shopping."

"Oh."

"Don't worry, there is a young man here who needs my help, only he doesn't know it."

How familiar that sounded!

"Thank you for the gift," she said, looking into his eyes and finding nothing but love there.

"You're welcome, daughter. How are things with you and Richard?" He grinned mischievously at her. "Now you know, Virginia, that everything happens for a reason. "

"You mean finally meeting you here has its purpose," she said.

"That, and other things."

"I want to have a child," she said suddenly. She knew it sounded abrupt, but she also knew that he would understand. He had always understood her, even when she wasn't thinking right.

"For what reason do you want a child?" he asked.

"What do you mean?" She hoped he wasn't reading her thoughts.

"I mean, a child is also a gift, a precious gift."

"And I deserve one."

"Be careful, Virginia."

Virginia could feel her face getting hot. If she'd touched it, it would have probably scalded her hand. She tried to remain peaceful, but the anger was seeping through her heart and out through her skin.

"Just remember what you've learned before."

"You mean about the stupid rocks."

God raised his left eyebrow and looked down the aisle. At the end of it stood a young man stocking shelves. "I must go to Trevor now," he said.

"But what about me?" It sounded wheezy and whiney but Virginia was bothered by God's treatment of her. It was if he didn't care. But that couldn't be it. He was still watching Trevor. She reached for him.

"Please, God, you've got to help me," she said.

But God didn't turn and she couldn't help watching the man in the brown corduroys and fisherman's cap walk slowly to the young man at the end of the aisle.

***

Virginia tossed the chocolate to the table. "I can't believe it," she said.

"Can't believe what?" Richard was just finishing with the last tray. "You got the chocolate."

"Of course I got the stupid chocolate!"

He didn't even have to turn. Virginia was angry about something...something else maybe, but possibly the same thing she'd been upset about for years.

"God, he's not going to help me."

Richard eyed her carefully. Had God finally come to her then? He was glad, but why was she so angry?

"I asked him for a child, to his very face, and he still wouldn't do it."

"Did he say why?"

"Something about a child being 'a precious gift' and that I needed to be 'careful.'"

Richard couldn't have been more shaken. Sure, he'd fully suspected that a child would never be in the realms of possibility for them, but now after Virginia's visit with God, things seemed definite.

He reached for Virginia and held her close. "So, what do you need to be careful about?" he asked.

"I guess asking God for something that I shouldn't be asking him about. I don't know. He seemed pretty frustrated with me. There was a boy there, someone stocking the shelves, and he seemed more concerned about him. Kind of left me standing there."

"Did he say anything else?"

"Nothing much. I was just reminded about the rocks; how I should remember them."

"Oh." Richard brushed at her hair but he didn't say anything. Still, his thoughts went to the stones again and what they represented. Listening to God, trusting in him, having optimism no matter your situation, being tenacious and never giving up and being constant with God through it all. Were they both doing that?

And then Richard thought of something else. Perhaps the cupcake with the ring in it had been a furtherance of learning so to speak. But what happened after a person was constant with God? He considered his talk with Virginia and went over the thoughts they'd spoken about.

The little girl had been helped by God, and he was committed to his wife in marriage. What did the two have in common?

Virginia was brushing away her tears and looking up at him. "So where are you?" she asked.

"Sorry. I was just thinking about the cupcake with the ring in it."

Virginia laughed. It was more of a cough with a laugh at the end, but it was something. "Kind of reminds you of the stone thing," she said.

***

Later that night Virginia noticed that Richard was reading his Bible. He sat in the corner chair by the lamp and appeared pretty intent on the words. She was watching her favorite program along with popcorn and a soda.

After a while it was hard to focus on the program. It was just eating at her, kind of like the hole in the couch. What could possibly be more interesting than what she was doing? She wasn't sure that she could ask him, though her thoughts wandered in his direction during commercials. The buttery smell of the popcorn filled her nostrils and the soda sparkled, just egging her on to take another sip. She did and then turned her attention back to her husband. He was still reading that stupid book.

Finally, she couldn't help it. "So what's so interesting?" she asked.

He looked up, smiled slightly, then put his nose back into the book. "Lots of things."

She was infuriated. "Like what?"

"Do you really want to know?"

She nodded her head, put another handful of popcorn into her waiting mouth, paused the show, and chewed.

"I've been wondering about the cupcake all day," he said, "especially after you returned." He paused for a moment, took his eyes from the Bible and looked directly at her.

"You know about constancy, but really, what do you think it means?"

"Being constant with God. It means you walk with him," she said.

"Right. But I think there's more."

She got a sudden chill up her arms and waited.

"Virginia, what do you think it means to be committed. I mean, really committed?"

She shrugged. "Why don't you tell me," she said.

"Walking with God is only part of it. God expects us to walk with him through good times and bad, right? And it's great when times are good. It's easier to walk with God."

Don't I know it, Virginia thought but didn't say.

"Listen to this: 'And they said, Go to. Let us build us a city and a tower, whose top may reach into heaven... (Genesis 11:4).' He looked up. "I've heard this story ever since I was a little boy but never really understood it. I knew that the people had built the tower to get into heaven; they thought they could climb it. But the only way to really get to heaven is to obey God."

"So?" Virginia's heart was beating quickly. *Why that scripture?*

"The people actually thought that if they put in some physical effort like building a tower, that nothing else would be required of them. They'd be in heaven

46

and they wouldn't have to do anything else. Remember what happened next?"

"God came down from heaven," Virginia said, "and he created more than one language." She stopped. "That's right, isn't it?"

"Yes, but why?"

"Well, if the people couldn't speak to one another they wouldn't be able to finish the tower."

"And maybe," Richard added, his eyes piercing her own, "just maybe they'd have to communicate with God so that he could help them to get to heaven. It's really about keeping the commandments."

Virginia rolled her eyes. "You sound just like a Sunday school lesson," she said. "I think I'll go back to my movie." She reached for the remote.

"Wait. Just a minute. Can you do that for me, honey?"

He'd been using the pet name 'honey' a lot recently. And she'd noticed something else. He seemed more kind, more sensitive of her. He wasn't as critical. "Okay, but just a minute. I want to finish my show."

Instead of reading from the chair, he stood, bringing the Bible with him. At the couch he sat next to her, his body turned slightly to the right so that he could see her. "Do you think we've been trying too hard? I mean, we put together that nursery, did all of the doctor testing and stuff, and spoke to each other as if we were going to get a child within the week."

"And what's wrong with that. That's optimism." *There, right in his face. What could he do now?*

He hesitated. So, she had got him. "You're right," he said, surprising her. "And then we followed the optimism with tenacity and constancy, and when nothing happened we stopped listening and trusting in God."

"That's right. We did what was required. We did what God wanted, and we were supposed to get the prize..." She stopped herself, for suddenly she was thinking about the precious gift that God had spoken to her about. Her heart seemed to stop. What was Richard saying?

"Don't you see, honey? We were building a tower to God. We thought if we did all of the right things we'd get to heaven."

"But shouldn't we, get there, I mean?"

"Not in the ways we were doing it. We were going through the motions, taking the steps, but we weren't drawing closer to God. We were building our own tower, thinking we could get there without him!"

Richard's face was flushed. He reached for her hand and squeezed her fingers. "God wants us to be committed to each other. We learned about that in our marriage vows. But he also wants us to be committed to him."

Richard stood, walked to the kitchen, and returned with the pink cupcake. He'd decided to save it against her wishes, and it was still pink but crusty from the outside air. He handed it to her.

"Commitments go two ways. We make a commitment to God and he makes a commitment to us. And though God always keeps his commitments we don't always keep them back."

"You're talking about me."

"And me."

"Well, I just don't see how we'll be able to keep all of the commandments. I mean, I had a hard enough time following the parable of the five stones, how in the world am I going to do more?"

"So that's it."

"What?" She handed him the cupcake and reached again for the remote.

"The stones. They became difficult because you were trying to use them on your own."

"I wasn't in the beginning."

"But later, what happened later?"

Virginia couldn't believe it. Her husband was right. She hadn't remembered. In her anger she'd forgotten God.

"You make is sound like the stones are a circular process, never ending. I guess I knew that."

"And forgot. We all forget." He wrapped her in his arms. "Why don't we start over?" he said, returning to his former position in front of her. "God gave us the cupcake lesson for a reason, and I'm bound and determined to find out what he wants for us."

The Choice

The talk with his wife had gone well. He hadn't planned it, and yet the timing had been perfect. A sudden warmth reached up his back and filtered to his heart. Things would be alright now, now that he and Virginia were on track.

They'd decided to pray together, and last night he'd taken the first shift. He'd spoken to God about being thankful for what they had; their business, his wife, his home, and had ended the prayer with even more thanks. He really couldn't be thankful enough for what he had.

Tonight was Virginia's turn. He wondered what she would say as they knelt beside their bed, clasped hands, and spoke with God. He wondered if she would do it.

But she was happy today; happier than he'd seen her in months; or had it been years? A new class was beginning the first week in February, a class for couples called, "Knowing Your Spouse's Heart," and

Virginia seemed excited about teaching it, though she had enrolled him in the class as well.

"It will be good for us," she'd explained. "I'm going to use some positive stuff I've learned through the years."

"The stones?"

"The stones AND the cupcake."

"It's fitting that we are holding the class next to the bakery," he'd said.

"There are no accidents," she'd answered.

***

"Dear God," Virginia prayed. "Please help us to know thy will. Please help us to know what to do next in finding our child. We are thinking that maybe we'd like a girl. Yes, a girl, but she doesn't need to be a baby. She could be like the little girl at *Just Desserts*. You know the one."

She felt Richard shift at her side. Maybe the prayer was wrong. Maybe she was doing it all wrong...

"And... God? Keep us safe until that time comes. Amen."

The prayer ended, Virginia didn't dare look into her husband's eyes. It had been so long since she'd prayed, and never in her life had she prayed out loud. She felt suddenly silly and insecure.

***

Virginia was nervous. There were only seven in the class, two returns, but all she could think about was who was sitting near the back. Perhaps he only wanted to make sure that she kept on track, or that the class was interesting...or something, but God was silent and it appeared that no one else saw him but herself.

She handed out the bags of stones, a treat that she figured others would appreciate. They weren't the expensive kind, of course, (she'd written the words on them herself) but there was something about remembering what to do when you had physical objects to look at.

"So how do you know your spouse's heart?" she asked, following the stone presentation. It had occurred to her that the stones were really a representation of a person's personal relationship with God and that this relationship must be somewhat in order to have a close marriage relationship – or the symbol of the cupcake.

There were a few nods of the head.

"I think I get the stones bit," said a woman in her mid-thirties. "I mean, you have to have a relationship with God, don't you, before you can really have a great relationship with your husband. But I don't see how a wife can see into her husband's heart, especially if he doesn't talk and when he does it's all about sports."

There was laughter from the group, and the only man in the class raised his hand.

"At least we're not emotional. I mean, women can't handle anything. It's like they have to have us men to support them, both financially and emotionally."

The woman's face in the front row turned a burnished red. "So, you're saying that without men we wouldn't be able to go on in life."

The man smiled and winked at her, which only disturbed the woman more.

"I really want this to be a positive experience," said Virginia. "My question has to do with men *and* women. How does a husband better understand his wife and his wife better understand her husband?"

A young woman raised her hand. "I would like my husband to see me better, I mean – really see me. You know that movie, 'Avatar?' I want it to be like that...'I see you...'"

The man coughed. Briefly, Virginia looked at the back of the room. God was still there but, like usual, she couldn't tell what he was thinking.

"So why weren't our spouses invited to this event?" asked another woman. She was heavy set, wore a flowered dress and spoke loudly, as if she wanted to make sure that everyone heard. "I want my husband to know what is happening so that you can fix him."

Virginia giggled with the rest of the class. But the woman appeared serious. "He is the worst husband on the planet. Always telling me what to do; never respecting my opinion..."

"I know just what you mean," suggested the young woman. "It's like I'm 'his woman' and I could never have a thought of my own. So what about inviting our spouse's next time? I would like that too. If he'll come, that is."

Virginia felt as if she was suddenly in an AA meeting; the class hadn't gone as she'd planned, and thoughts of having double the number next week disturbed her more than she wanted to let on. She looked towards the back of the room.

God was gone.

***

"What?" Richard was laughing, his sides breathing in and out like bagpipes. "So, did you finish the class, or what?"

"We...finished."

"Well?" He was sitting on the living room couch and they were sharing a bowl of popcorn. Dinner had been a bust. She'd been so worried about the class that she'd burnt the lasagna. At least the popcorn had turned out.

"I don't know if I can say it."

"What...what?" He stopped eating and touched her leg. "Whatever you say won't faze me, I promise."

"This will. The only man in the room got so fed up with the ladies that he walked out! Can you believe it? He said, 'This is the dumbest class I've ever attended,' and he walked out."

"What did you do?" He reached his hand into the bowl.

"What do you mean, what did I do? I didn't do anything, I just continued the class. It went much better after he left."

"Well, maybe the idea of having both spouses there is a good idea," he said. "It is a class on marriage."

"I know." She took another bite, feeling pretty stupid that she hadn't thought of that in the first place. But then again, life did nothing but show her what was working...and what wasn't on a continual basis.

***

Richard reached for the pink cupcake.

"The ring isn't like the last one," the little girl said, but she licked the frosting off of the top, working her tongue around the ring that was still planted there. "My mom won't like it."

"These are special cupcakes, too," said Richard, walking around the counter and bending so he could be at her eye level. The girl had green eyes, the color of deep satin, but her cheeks were ruddy and red. It was still cold out. She wore an old coat, torn at the sleeve. The coat was dirty almost everywhere else. Her blond hair was clean, as was her face before the licking of the cupcake. Richard noticed she had a pink oval around her tiny lips. She was licking the sides of it.

"So, there was a real diamond in the last cupcake."

"Must have been a mistake," the girl offered, licking another section of the cupcake.

"No mistake. So, the money has been spent already?"

"No, but I wanted to get prepared. Mom says that she wants to be prepared for the invetable."

The ring came off the top of the cupcake, was licked and then placed on her forefinger like before.

"I think you mean inevitable," Richard said.

"Yeah, that."

"So where is your mom going?"

The little girl blinked over at him and in that moment, Richard took greater notice. "My name is Richard," he said.

"Joy," said the little girl, taking her first bite.

The Feast – A Parable of the Ring

***

It was Saturday and Virginia was home working on the guest room. It felt sort of funny calling it that, but Virginia knew that changing the room, including the yellow paint, would only help her to heal.

She'd decided on an eggshell white with lavender accents. They'd purchased a twin bed, new end tables, new drapes for the windows and plenty of pillows. These were placed lovingly on the bed and reminded Virginia of something from the Victorian era. The color was subtle, calming and reflective.

A chair with a lavender cushion stood in the corner of the room along with a small desk for writing and the closet had been decked out with the latest shelving.

Virginia couldn't help smiling. The room was beautiful after all, and she was doing much better. She walked to the window. All the clutter had been removed and disposed of weeks before but she could still see it there, clustered on the snow that would one day melt to make room for spring.

As she continued to look out the window, she saw a neighborhood child look up at her and wave. Virginia smiled and waved back. It made her heart fill with warmth and a little loneliness. Perhaps, after all, it was unfair of her to think she would never have children.

***

Richard was grinning from ear to ear. "Really? You really mean it?"

"I don't think it would hurt."

"I didn't think you wanted to adopt."

Virginia paced the living room. "I didn't think so either, but maybe this is the answer. If we can't have children, maybe the Lord wants us to adopt."

"Are you sure, I mean, what about the whole thing with carrying a baby and having it be our own..."

Virginia waved her hand. "Come see what I did today," she said.

Richard followed her into the guest room. It was beautifully done, all the way to the throw pillows. "Wow. It looks like something from a magazine."

"So, what do you think about bringing the little girl here?" she asked.

"A girl? You want to adopt a girl?"

"I think so," said Virginia. "No, I know so."

She walked to the bed, caressed the pillows and sat down. "I think this would be a perfect room for a little girl."

***

The choice wasn't an easy one, but Virginia was happier now than ever and Richard, well – he was beside himself with joy. Joy, that was her name, wasn't it?

He pictured the little girl with the golden hair and green eyes in the room, and imagined her sleeping in her bed and cuddling her favorite stuffed animal. They didn't have any toys yet, but once they found out her age then the problem would be rectified.

Richard got on his knees with his wife and together they prayed for the little girl that would soon be theirs. Virginia prayed that all would go well, that the girl would come without trouble and that she would be happy with them.

"Dear God, we know this is the right thing, and we know you will support us in this worthy desire. Amen."

There was something about the prayer that disturbed him, but he shrugged it off. Virginia was glowing and Richard, well – he was beyond joy.

* * *

The terrible dream awoke her. She had been fitfully chasing a little girl with golden hair. Joy continued to climb the mountain away from Virginia's waiting hands.

"What is it?"

Richard sat up. "Have a bad dream?" he asked. Today was the day they were going to visit the Tucked in Tight Adoption Agency in Idaho Falls. Today was the day her dream was to be realized.

As she got ready, she watched Richard from the corner of her eye. He was as excited as she was.

"Ouch!"

"What did you do now?" she asked.

"Nicked myself again. Can you grab me a tissue?"

The tissue in hand, Richard stuck a small piece on his chin. "I don't know about you but I'm a nervous wreck."

Kathryn Elizabeth Jones

She smiled, wrapping the colorful scarf around her neck. It would be good for their future child to see her in a bit of color. "Do you think it will be quick?" she asked.

He shrugged. "We can only hope. Anyway, we need some time to pick up those toys you talked about."

"Yeah, but not until we see her. We also will need to know her clothing sizes and what she enjoys doing."

"Have you thought about an age?"

"Six or seven? I'd like to get a girl that's young enough that we have some say in the matter."

He looked at her squarely. "What matter?"

"I've heard that some children are abused. I'm not sure I could take on a girl like that."

"Like what?" He wiped his face with a towel and watched her through the glass. "Whatever she's been through, we'll get her through it. How bad could it be?"

Virginia thought about her dream. "I don't know," she said. "Are you sure we're doing the right thing?"

"Oh, no, no, you're not going to back out now."

"I'm not...backing out as you say...it's just that..."

"What?"

"What if we don't know how to be parents? What if a baby would be better, then we wouldn't have to worry about so much stuff."

Richard touched her on the arm. "We'll be great parents. As for getting an older child we've already talked about that. It takes months, sometimes years to

59

get a baby, but an older child will cut down the waiting time. Besides, you've changed over the room."

Virginia shrugged. "I know, but I'm just worried. What if they won't take us as parents?"

"You mean the agency?"

She nodded.

"Why wouldn't they take us? We're healthy, we make enough money to support a child...we..."

"We're old. At last look I'm 40 and you're a mere 42."

"So?"

"So maybe they don't want old people adopting children."

"I can't believe it. You don't actually think our ages will keep us from adopting our girl?"

She shrugged, brushing back her blond hair from her face. It had grown longer since she'd been married, and curled naturally down her back. "I don't know, I'm just worried."

"You already said that."

***

"Remember, this is a great opportunity," he said.

The huge red brick house in front of them seemed to speak of times long gone but difficult to let go of. Virginia had thoughts she had no idea how to express. They'd said a prayer that morning about getting a girl and being good parents. They'd left the house with high hopes and a myriad of questions.

At least, that was the case with Virginia.

She wasn't sure that Richard was right but she believed he was, and as the doors of the old house loomed before them, Virginia considered how boxed in she'd been.

She'd been single for most of her life, had spent her time primarily indoors and now – now she was married and going places she'd never dreamed she would visit. Still, as Richard opened the door, they entered a warm visiting area that could only be thought of as a home away from home. She and Richard stepped inside, as ready as they'd ever be for what wonders would come next.

***

The woman before them smiled hesitantly. Her short, dark hair hit at chin level, and her wide face and glasses gave her that 'please don't disturb me' look. And yet, here she was interviewing them as if this was her talent in life. Her business tag revealed her name: Sandy. It seemed like an appropriate name for someone dealing with the grit of matching up families.

"I see from your paperwork that you are married and that you both have jobs, but are one of you ready to leave your career to be home with a child?"

"We've already discussed that," said Richard. "Virginia will be home with the child."

"No desires to pursue school?"

"Not at my age," said Virginia.

"As for your age..." The woman looked at Virginia. Richard pictured some sort of dinosaur before attack. "Are you concerned that your age will cause a problem in the future...with a baby..."

"Actually, we're wanting a girl, an older girl, so that should take a few years off and give us a better head start," Richard joked.

The woman didn't laugh. Richard could see distinct frown lines on either side of her face. Sure, she was probably sixty or so, but still..."

"It usually takes a year or so to get a baby, but since you are opting for a child and a girl, we may be able to fit you with a child sooner. You have already paid the application fee but we will need to set up a home study. Are you considering adopting internationally or domestically?"

Richard turned to Virginia. "We haven't talked about that," he said.

Sandy looked down at the paperwork. "Well, after you do, you'll have to finish this, but consider how an international child might be best for you because of your ages. Actually, an international child is usually harder to adopt. But please, please, don't decide that now. Get back to me in the next few days with your answer."

She handed them back their forms, including a couple of others she suggested they both look at. "These must be filled out completely before we can proceed."

Richard realized that they'd forgotten to check the appropriate box. No wonder the woman had been a bit, well, stiff. He looked over at Virginia and handed her the papers. "Then, we'll be back soon," he said, "after we've made our decision."

Sandy stood. "There are many children needing a home. Usually boys are adopted first, and girls, sadly, only about half as often. I am happy that you've made this decision." Sandy tried to smile, but like before it was restrained, though her handshake was firm.

***

It was just easier not to think about it. As Virginia paced the house she thought of the challenges they might have adopting a child outside of the U.S.

There was so much red tape! She gaped at the list Sandy had given her of laws, processes, home study information; even what to expect following the adoption. It made her head swirl.

Was this the right answer?

It was Saturday and Richard was at work. The pink cupcakes were selling marvelously, and many couples had discovered the find. Just yesterday one couple had given her an order for 250. "We're going to use these for the guests instead of a wedding cake."

The idea was cute and Virginia had smiled at the couple before telling them about her new class. It was going alright, but Virginia was missing something, though she wasn't sure what. She'd involved both spouses, but the arguing had continued. Richard continued to attend, breaking up minor squabbles as necessary, and getting the group back on task.

And then he'd come up with an idea.

"I think you need a booklet," he said. "Sort of a working guide. And what about writing love letters, sharing thoughts about what is working in the marriage; sort of a positive motivation project."

It was a good idea, though Virginia wondered why she hadn't thought of it first. She was a woman after all, and didn't women usually have the heart to think of all that mushy, close-knit stuff?

God was no longer attending her classes, but the thought that he was still there knowing what she was doing worried and comforted her at the same time.

Would he like what she was doing?

Though the five stones were beginning to gather power again within her mind and heart, Virginia was also thinking of the pink cupcake and diamond ring and how much the symbol was beginning to mean to her.

Had Richard been right? Was the cupcake more than a sweet treat – a way to understand the commitment they'd made to each other? Commitments came in all sorts and included the commitment a mother had to a child and God had to his children.

And then a new thought came to Virginia. It was about the tower, about climbing to heaven, and she felt ashamed. That was what she was doing, making a commitment to God and then doing it all on her own. Sure, she got his help sometimes, but only at the expense of the tower. That's why she had fixed up the room for the baby, gone through all of those tests, visited various doctors; she had been living and breathing optimism and tenacity, and wasn't that being constant with God?

Of course, she'd missed the first two steps, and was continually forgetting about listening and trust, but they were the hardest stones for her – the ones that took the most effort to be with God and to walk with him.

Walking to the kitchen Virginia grabbed the stale cupcake and tossed it into the garbage. It was turning a sickly white-pink anyway, and the ring was stuck in the cupcake for all time.

***

Richard reached for the newly frosted chocolate cake and handed it to God. "And what would you want with a chocolate cake?" he asked.

"As I told you before, sometimes chocolate is my favorite."

God paid for the purchase, which appeared strange to Richard; and God picked up the cake. "Before long it will be spring even in the mountains," he said. "And you know what spring brings."

It was more of a statement than a question but Richard got the gist. "I guess I should be watching for flowers," he said.

"And other things," said God. "But I don't want you to be too disappointed. Just have an open mind, keep praying and allowing me to be a part of your life. Can you do that?"

Richard nodded. A sudden lump had grown in his throat.

***

"So, what did he say?"

Richard plunked the bag of groceries on the counter. She reached inside and began pulling things out.

"Oh, you know – stuff that we're going to need to get us through this challenging time."

Virginia turned to him. "So what specifically did he say?"

***

Virginia considered Richard's words as she cleaned up the house. It sounded as if things were going to be harder than they'd anticipated. Would the adoption take longer than expected? Once they'd been chosen, the waiting time would be roughly a year. Would they be waiting even longer? What if the child had a problem of some kind and they'd have to deal with physical or emotional issues? What if the child was a boy?

The sudden thought made her gasp. Just because they wanted a girl, that didn't mean that's what God wanted for them. What would they do with a boy? A chill raced up Virginia's back.

The mop stopped in the corner. Well, if it was a boy, then they'd just do the same things. Except boys liked different things and they played much rougher. But they weren't as catty as girls, so that had to be a plus. Still...

"What if we get a boy?"

"But we've asked for a girl." The words coming from the other end of the cell phone were just like she remembered of Richard, before he'd made some slight adjustments that had brought life and a renewed love into their home.

"I know that." The mop was propped now and she was sitting on the old couch with the hole in it. "What would you do if you knew God wanted you to adopt a boy instead of a girl."

There was a pause, far too long for the previous Ms. Virginia Bean.

"Well?"

"If that's what God wants us to have, then we'll get a boy. Right?"

Virginia sighed with relief. "That's what I thought. So what if it's also a boy and he has, you know, problems."

"What kind of problems?"

"Maybe he is...I don't know, different."

"We're all different. Does that really matter?"

Virginia considered Richard's words. Did it matter? Did any of it really matter? They were going to have child, and healthy or not, they would be parents.

***

"So, you're saying you want to change the forms," asked Sandy. She had that straight face that Richard hated.

"My wife and I (and God, he thought to himself) have considered the importance of keeping things open. We'll take and love a boy or a girl; we've even considered adopting a child with difficulties."

"What sort of difficulties?" asked the case worker.

"Well," Richard looked toward his wife. They had discussed them all. Autism. Cerebral palsy. Aids. Down Syndrome...

"It says here that you don't have any other children. Usually families with biological children will choose to adopt a child with disabilities simply because they've had the experience of raising children and the adopted child will have older siblings to help him or her out. They feel as experienced parents they have something to offer a child with disabilities. Of course, no matter which child you receive, there will be adjustments. We talked about this before..."

Richard remembered. There was the issue of abuse and neglect, drug addiction by a mother passed on to the infant...the list went on and on...He turned to his wife: "I really thought we'd figured this one out," he said.

"Well, this isn't like buying a loaf of bread," Sandy interrupted, standing up. She paced the room as she spoke. "A child is a special gift, and what you want and know you can handle must be carefully discussed. You wouldn't want to make the wrong decision."

"Has that ever happened?" Richard asked.

The woman turned and replanted herself in the swivel chair. "Of course it's happened, and it's quite disturbing I can tell you, but you need to know that we do all in our power to weed out the undesirables." She paused. Richard's heart thundered. Who was this woman? And why was she working at an adoption agency?

"Of course, if you fill out all of the required forms appropriately, there should be only minor problems that every adoptive parent has to work through. I don't want you to worry about it." A rigid smile. "Just make those decisions and get back to me."

She stood again, ushering them out.

***

Weeks later they'd opened the door even further.

"So, you're considering a baby as well?" Sandy asked, pushing her glasses back on her nose. "Are you sure about that?"

Virginia felt the chills up her arms and knew it was the right decision. "I'm sorry," she said, "but we really need to be open to what God wants for us."

The woman smiled. It was the first real smile Virginia had seen.

"Well then. I'll open it up then as you say. Put together some letters and photos and I'll get these promptly in the binder. All the girls go through them when deciding on the parents for their baby."

She stood and walked to the window. "We'll keep things open, and see what happens, alright?"

When she turned, she was still smiling and Virginia couldn't help it. She was smiling too.

***

Virginia stood in the center of the kitchen. Well, it was the best she could do. The cupboards had been polished to a shine, the floor mopped, the counters wiped until they gleamed. She'd even done some deep cleaning to make sure everything was in order both visually and behind cupboard doors.

And she and Richard had had to pay for the home study visit from Sandy. $2,000 wasn't a mere pittance, and Virginia hoped that all the money forked out would be worth it. The bottom line?

She hoped she passed.

The Feast – A Parable of the Ring

***

The moment God walked around the corner, Richard knew he was in trouble. "Virginia needs you," he said. "You haven't taken any of her calls."

Actually, Virginia hadn't called him. His phone hadn't rung once, had it? Richard's thoughts whirled. So, God knew his wife was in trouble and he wasn't going to lift a finger to help her?

"It's you that must help her."

Richard placed the newly baked cookies under the counter. He was suddenly more worried than he could explain. He looked up. "I'm sorry," he said. "I'll go right now."

***

The room was shuttered dark. The blinds were closed. Virginia sat on the bed, wiping at her eyes. She had done everything right, and now this. She blinked and a tear slid down her cheek. She thought of the child, the boy or girl that might never come. And she was afraid.

What if she'd blown everything?

They'd recently painted fluffy white clouds on the ceiling, and as Virginia watched them, she could imagine the wind ripping by and pushing them along. In time the clouds would be gone and she'd see blue sky again.

Was she making a big deal out of nothing?

"Virginia!" The call came from the front of the house. Richard.

"I'm back here!" she sobbed back, wiping at her tears. She'd called him numerous times on the phone without an answer, and now he was here. "In the baby's room!" She'd said it without thinking; as if she'd never torn down the crib, the drapes, or scattered the clothing. But the room was beautiful now, fit for a child, though probably not a boy.

"Virginia!" Richard raced into the room. "How are you?" He scanned her face and drew her to him. "What's going on?"

"The home study."

Richard sniffed. "Smells like the cleanest house on the planet," he said.

"I wish Sandy thought the same."

He pulled her from him and looked into her eyes.

"It went alright, didn't it?"

A sudden sound like a branch scraping against the window, startled her. "Yes, I mean no..."

"No and yes?"

He was frustrated, she could tell.

"She was happy at first. Thought the place was spruced up nicely..."

"And?"

Virginia wiped at her nose. She didn't have a tissue. "She was angry about us not having a fire extinguisher. 'That was on the paper I gave you,' she said. And then she complained about us not having outlet covers...I don't even remember seeing that one on the list."

"Outlet covers?" Richard asked, aghast.

"Can you believe she wiped her hand over every piece of furniture to make sure that there were no sharp edges? I don't even want to speak about the hole in the sofa."

"Holy cow."

"Not only that, she asked about the parent training classes. I told her we hadn't been to any of them yet. The first one started last week. I guess I forgot."

"We haven't even been chosen yet. I thought the class came later. How many of them do we have to go to?"

Virginia looked at the paper by her side. She'd picked it up right after Sandy had left her. "Four."

"Then we'll go to the next four," said Richard. "Anything else?"

"Well, just this one thing."

Richard sat waiting. She fingered the comforter.

"The garage. Seems there's some hazardous stuff low enough for a child to reach."

"Oh. Well then, I'll need to get to it. I'll do it this Saturday."

"You work this Saturday."

"No, you work this Saturday."

***

Virginia had just finished cleaning the outsides of the counter when she saw him.

"So, how are you doing today?" he asked. This time he had a small girl at his right holding his hand. She looked just like the little girl she'd seen out the lavender window.

72

"Miss Joy here, she would like one of your pink cupcake's, please."

So it was the little girl. Virginia tried not to stare, but the girl was beautiful. She had striking blond hair and green eyes. She was petite and her dress was a bit baggy for her small frame, but she was still captivating. She wore a pink sweater and scuffed, black shoes. No tights.

She reached for the cupcake and handed it to the child. "How old are you?" she asked.

"Ten."

A small girl for ten, Virginia thought but didn't say. "So, why do you like pink cupcakes so much?" she asked.

Joy looked up at God. Her eyes said everything.

God reached into his pocket and pulled out some change. He laid it on the counter. "Take what you need," he said, "the rest can go to Miss Joy here."

The girl smiled and hugged him, but not before mashing some of the frosting onto his shirt. The child didn't seem to notice and neither did God. Virginia took the few remaining coins and placed them in the front pocket of Joy's dress. God touched Virginia briefly on the arm and then he turned with the child.

"Thank you, Virginia," he said.

***

Richard coughed. The dust in the garage was thicker than fog. It bothered him in more ways than he could say. What did it matter if the garage wasn't sparkling clean? He'd lock the door or something – keep the child out. He'd bought shelving, brackets, bins to keep everything in, and his arms were beginning to cramp up from all of the lifting.

It was noon already and today he'd remembered to turn his cell phone on – the problem of a few days ago when Virginia hadn't been able to reach him. He couldn't forget that one ever again, especially after the child arrived.

The shelves up, he reached for the first bin. It slid nicely on the shelf. He reached for the second. Each bin was already full of tools, ropes or other supplies. He even had a bin for camping gear – actually he had three of them. He reached for the last bin. This one held memorabilia; his wife's. He was tempted to look inside but didn't. Instead, he placed the last bin on the shelf and turned back to his work.

When the same bin came crashing down seconds later, Richard was beyond patience. "What?" he screamed, though no one was there to hear him. "Why couldn't you stay on board like the others?" He bent down and reached for the various cards, letters and photos. Grabbing them by the fistful's he'd gathered most of it when he saw the photo.

It was Virginia alright, and next to her, Paul. They held each other in a warm embrace. Virginia was kissing him on the lips. The photo was small – a black and white, and like one of those taken at those instant photo places one might see at a carnival or mall.

Virginia had spoken about Paul like an old friend, but as Richard's eyes scanned the two letters he'd discovered within the memorabilia he realized something else. Virginia had been in love with Paul and Paul had been in love with Virginia.

A sudden sadness filled his heart, though he knew that Paul was dead. He placed the photo and the letters inside the bin and sat it again on the high shelf.

***

"Wow! The place looks beautiful!" shrieked Virginia when she saw it. "You even got my memory box up there."

Richard's heart pounded. "Yeah, I was even able to manage that."

"You say it like it was heavy or something."

"No...it was just the last one and I was tired," Richard said. "Let's go inside and get something to eat."

***

Richard was jealous. No, he was angry. The poor guy was dead but he was still angry. The letters had been stunning, almost too perfect, and the two had obviously been in love.

There had been a "connection," a "bonding" that Paul had spoken about in the two letters Richard had found. And strangely enough, he'd discovered hearts on the edges of the letters. It was all he could do to eat dinner.

"So, the garage. How long did it take you?" Virginia asked.

Richard took a loaded bite of spaghetti. The noodles slid down his throat like unspoken lies. How could he tell her what he'd found and how he felt about what he'd found? She would think him stupid.

Anyway, why would he find those letters and photo now, and why would he care about them?

"Well?"

Richard realized he hadn't answered. "About half the day," he said, though it had taken him longer. The reading of the letters had taken him about an hour. He'd read them over and over until he almost knew them by heart. He was embarrassed, but keenly aware that Virginia was staring at him.

"Something is wrong," she finally said. "Tell me. I have done plenty of crying and temper tantrums for the both of us. Did Sandy call or something?"

He shook his head.

"Then what?"

The idea of telling her revolted him. Jealousy was something that happened the first couple of years in marriage – if it happened at all. He could hardly believe he was thinking it.

"I dumped your box inside the garage."

Her fork with noodles and sauce rested in mid-air. "None of it got ruined, did it?"

He gulped. "No."

She took a bite. "I didn't see anything on the garage floor. Thanks for picking them up."

"You're welcome." He took another loaded bite of spaghetti and another. The garlic bread rested near his plate. He picked it up, dipped it in the sauce and took a bite. The bread was tasty, and the garlic perfect.

"You're awfully quiet."

He took another bite of spaghetti, and another until the plate was empty except for a bit of sauce. He finished the garlic bread.

"Wow, I've never seen you eat like that," she said, leaning in. "So, what is it?"

"I... I saw some stuff in that box."

"Naturally." She was grinning at him, but she didn't know his thoughts. He wondered how she'd respond if she knew.

"Well, there was a picture and some letters."

"I know. It is my box."

"You. And Paul."

"So that's it."

"What?" He wiped his mouth with the napkin.

"You're jealous. I didn't think you had a jealous bone in your body."

"Neither did I." He stood, taking his plate to the sink and washing it off.

"So?"

"So, I found it, and instead of putting them back I read them. I'm sorry."

"You what?"

He turned to see her fragile face staring up at him. She'd pulled her long blond hair back today and the style emphasized her eyes. They were even larger. He didn't answer her immediately and she was silent. All Richard could think about was taking every word back. That was until she said, "You know, that commitment stuff is really starting to sink in. Imagine, a man who I thought didn't have a sliver of jealousy in his body has some after all."

"It's embarrassing."

"No, it's not." She stood and walked to the sink with her own dish. "I like it that you have flaws other than leaving your clothes all over the place. But mostly, I like that you are committed enough to me to tell me about them."

***

With the paperwork in and the additional items checked off of their list, she and Richard reached the doors. Today was the day of their first class.

Her heart was beating like a thunderstorm but she tried to maintain an exterior of calmness and courage, for she would need a lot of courage to get through this one. The class was full, not a chair remained, and as she and Richard stood at the back, Sandy motioned them over.

"There are more chairs in the next classroom. Do you mind getting a couple?"

Richard nodded and left the room, while Virginia stood waiting.

In the meantime, she surveyed the people in the room. Most were young; a couple had young children with them already, and one couple in particular looked about the ages of she and her husband. But they were sitting up at the front.

Richard returned with the folding chairs. He sat them up in the back.

"Let's begin then," said Sandy, as if on cue. "Most of you know me as one of the case workers here, but I also teach some pretty inspiring parenting classes."

The room was quiet.

Richard nudged her. "I can't believe she said that," he whispered, then turned his face toward the front. Virginia got the distinct impression that Sandy had heard him. But from way up front?

"As you probably know from the flyer, today I'll be speaking about beliefs and attitudes as they relate to adoption. The second part of today I will be focusing on mental preparation." She tried to smile. "If, during my presentation, you have any questions, please don't hesitate to ask."

Virginia thought of her marriage class and hoped she didn't sound as dry.

Richard nudged her again, but she pretended to ignore him.

"We will also cover diaper changing. For those of you already experienced in this skill, I expect you will help the others." She looked directly at Virginia as if she thought that somehow she would be a likely candidate for either option.

Richard laughed. She nudged him back.

"We'll start with a short film." The room was darkened and Richard touched her leg in a romantic gesture. This was sure to be an enlightening experience.

***

The next few weeks were miserable. With the paperwork finished for the adoption agency, it was time for the waiting game, and that included saving a bit more money than they'd first expected.

Tonight she was giving her last class and she was excited about the cupcakes she'd baked with the diamond rings on top. It was to be their last hurrah, and Virginia was excited about the prospect of letting go of the class and allowing God to take each couple forward.

The next day she got a call from Sandy. "Can you come in to the office right away?" she asked. She sounded excited.

"Sure."

"I'll be in the office until 6. Just make sure you make it in by then."

Virginia turned to Richard. They were both working at *Just Desserts*. "Sandy wants to see us," she said.

"Both of us?" Richard was busy with a customer. There was a line and Virginia had only just dashed in-between customers to pick up the phone. She eyed the woman who was next in line and turned back to her husband. "Why don't I help you for a bit and then I'll go when things die down." She walked to the counter. "What can I help you with?" she asked.

The woman smiled wearily. She wore a thin coat and a dirty, crocheted hat, but her smile was warm. "I just want to thank you," she said.

Virginia blinked.

"I mean, it isn't every day that someone gives you a ring."

Virginia was silent as she watched the woman stare at her. She had the most vivid blue eyes, but her face was lined with worry. "I want to thank you for the diamond ring in the cupcake."

"But it wasn't me," Virginia said.

"I know." The woman wiped at her brown hair, pulling a few strands away from her face. "That's what Joy said..."

"God has a way of helping his children," Virginia said.

"Through other people. Joy has such faith in God."

A warmth like sunlight caressed Virginia's back. "I know. You have a beautiful little girl."

"Thank you." She turned.

"Can I get something for you?" Virginia asked.

"Oh, no, no. But thank you again."

As Virginia watched the woman, she couldn't help noticing the young blond girl standing nearby. Her mother had evidently asked her to wait by the last cash register in order for her not to overhear the conversation. But there was something about the little girl's face that told Virginia she'd somehow heard.

***

Virginia sat across the desk. Sandy smiled that crooked smile she was fond of. She pushed a colorful sheet of paper across the counter. Virginia looked down. It was the photos and letters she and Richard had written a few weeks ago.

"You must need an edit," she said, feeling discouraged again and not up for any more paperwork.

"Not an edit. I just wanted you to know that your profile has been taken out of the binder."

"My profile? Why?"

"Because someone has chosen you."

The Feast – A Parable of the Ring

The Feast

"Richard, Richard!" The scream seemed hollow in the large classroom, but as Virginia reached the counter her voice stopped at Richard's chest. The place was vacant for a change. Perfect, it would give them a moment to celebrate.

"We've been chosen!" Virginia shrieked.

"Chosen for what?"

"As parents, you dummy!" She didn't tell him that she'd been wandering in the same clueless darkness only an hour earlier.

"You mean, we're getting a child?"

Virginia smiled and hugged him. "Not just any child," she breathed, and the scent of Irish Spring filled her nostrils. "A baby girl."

***

"We need a crib, clothes and everything, everything I threw out the window."

"Yes, and what about bottles..."

"That's right bottles..." Virginia was making a list and her hands couldn't move fast enough.

"What about the girl. When do we meet her?"

"The girl? When she's born, of course."

He nudged her. "The girl who is having our baby," he said.

Virginia shrugged. "Oh, that girl. I think Sandy said next week or so. She's scheduling a meeting."

"Stop." He held out his hand so Virginia knew he was serious. He'd become much more serious the last few weeks as they'd prepared their minds for the child they wanted. "Can the girl change her mind after meeting us? What is her name anyway?"

"Gail Shepherd...I think."

"You think?" He stared at her incredulously. She felt her stomach turn. He was stressing her out. Suddenly she didn't feel very well.

"Well, I was so excited about being a mother that I didn't hear much of what the case worker said." She paused, looked up from the list, and smiled over at him. "Really, I'm sorry. I'll call her tomorrow, okay?"

He touched her hand. "You're not going to like what I'm going to say. I don't think we should make a list yet."

"Why not?"

"Because, honey, if she does change her mind we'll have a nursery once again without a child. You sure she said it was a girl?"

"Of course, I'm sure!" She threw the list at him and the pen whirled to the other side of the room.

**

Richard was worried. So, Virginia wasn't going to talk to him – again. So be it. He had plenty of work, plenty to do to keep his mind off of the situation...

He looked up.

"Hello."

"Hello, Richard. Heard the news about the baby."

"You too?"

God chuckled. "Well, actually..."

Richard felt suddenly stupid. "Sorry," he said. "I'm just worried about her, that's all."

"As well you should. She really wants to buy those clothes, and I think she's already picked out a crib."

"Is that so."

"Why are you so worried?"

"I'm not worried." In the very mention of worry Richard felt guilty. If anyone knew when he was feeling guilty it would be God. "Sorry," he said again.

"Stop saying sorry and do something about it," he said.

"I have no idea what to do. She thinks...I can't believe what she thinks."

"Tell me."

Richard looked into God's eyes for the very first time on this visit, and he liked what he saw there. Virginia was right. God did love him.

"She wants to buy everything and I'm afraid it's just not going to happen."

"What makes you say that?"

Richard looked past God but there wasn't anyone waiting for service. He turned his eyes back to him. "What if the girl changes her mind? It's been known to happen. I don't know if I can go through all of that again. Wouldn't it be better to hold off, just until we knew for sure?"

"It would be easier," said God.

"So, you agree."

"It would be easier. Consider the path you have trod up until this point. Hasn't everything served as instruction?"

Richard thought about God's words. Well, sure. He'd married Virginia and they had spent years trying to have a child. He understood Virginia better now than he'd done when they'd first met. He understood marriage better. He'd learned about patience, the importance of really seeing his wife and doing for her; yes, he'd even learned a bit about jealousy – why it didn't work in a marriage. He'd also learned about God and the relationship he needed to have with him, and combined, the relationship he needed to have with God and his wife.

"Those are some good thoughts," God said, placing his large hands on the counter and clasping them together. "But there is more yet to learn."

"You mean that Virginia just doesn't get it? Here she is doing exactly what she did the first time for a baby that might not even come."

"Where is your faith?"

"Well, at least I'm being realistic. At least I know what end is up."

"And what end is up, Richard?"

Richard eyed God closely but all he could see in God's eyes was love.

***

"I'm sorry," said Richard, taking his wife's hand. "What do you want to buy first?"

Virginia couldn't believe it. "You mean you'll go with me to get the crib and all the other stuff?"

Richard nodded. "Anything you want. I love you, honey."

Virginia hugged him. "You're a good man," she said, breathing into his ear, "but I don't want to buy a crib."

"She'll need a crib..."

"Look, we can wait awhile. Let's meet with Gail; get to know her a bit. We have plenty of time to get everything. Remember, we did this once before so now we have some practice. Imagine how fast we can purchase things this time around."

"Are you sure? What changed your mind?"

Virginia smiled, and pulled him to her again. "Let's just say I had a little talk with God."

***

Gail was a bright girl. She sat across from them at the adoption agency and read again from Richard's letter:

"'...Children come from the Lord and I want to be a good father to one of God's children.'" Gail looked up, a small tear traveling down her left cheek. Her stomach was round, and her blond hair was brushed back from her eyes in a large ponytail. "I think that's what did it," she said. "It was the part about God."

Richard looked at her, smiled, and patted her hand. It was a sweet gesture.

"I mean, I didn't want to get pregnant but now that I am, I'm happy to be giving my baby girl to such spiritual minded people. You will make good parents."

"Thank you," said Virginia. "We'll do our best."

"And I don't want you to get worried. You know, I won't change my mind, and I won't decide to keep it or anything."

Virginia's heart pounded. She looked over at Richard. His face had suddenly gone pale.

"Really. I am planning on going to college. My boyfriend...well, that's another story, but I'm going to make something of myself. I'm going to learn stuff."

"What are you going to major in?"

Gail shrugged her slim shoulders. "I'm not sure yet, but I've always been interested in bugs. I used to collect them as a kid. Maybe there's a major for that."

Richard smiled.

"And you." She turned to Virginia. "I like that you have blond hair. The father has blond hair, too, so there's a pretty good chance..."

"I can hardly believe it," said Virginia. "I feel so honored."

"You don't need to cry. Besides, the baby will be beautiful and you can cry then, after I have it." A sudden crinkle in the girl's forehead made Virginia wince. She was only 15 and she was going to have a baby.

***

It was the fourth week of their classes, and he and Virginia had already learned about coping after the adoption. They'd learned about the adoption triad, a sort of triangle representing the birth parent, the adopted child and the adoptive parents; the rite of passage and life art of raising an adopted child, and the intertwined culture and positive imagery necessary when times got hard.

Richard considered what he had learned, and he counted his relationship with God as his greatest asset. For wasn't it God that had brought he and his wife together and wasn't it God who was now engineering this new life into their lives?

"Now, I don't want you to get discouraged," Sandy was saying. "There will be times when you will need a time out. You will need to leave the room and let the baby cry."

"I could never do that," whispered Virginia to Richard.

"It won't hurt the baby to cry a little. And if your spouse is at home with you, this is also a good time for him to do a bit of helping. Any questions?"

Virginia raised her hand. "I just don't think I could let my baby cry," she said.

"That's well and good, but consider how much work you'll be doing on a daily basis and how tired you're going to be after a long day. Leaving the room is always better than picking up a baby when you are angry or tired."

"But I would never..."

Richard nudged her. "I think what's important here," said the case worker, "is that you know your limits for the protection of your new baby or child. It's important that you listen to the warning signs that we discussed. Any other questions?"

The Feast – A Parable of the Ring

"Are we finished?" shouted someone in the back.

Sandy blushed. "Almost. I have brought some treats as a thank you for your participation. I know you will all make great parents. If you ever have any concerns, please don't hesitate to call me." She opened the boxes on the table and reached for the juice.

***

"So, what do you think?" Gail patted her round belly. She was eight months along and the time was nearing. "Do you think she will be a soccer player or a ballerina?"

"Soccer player...ballerina," she and Richard echoed in unison, making Gail laugh. They were out on a picnic of sorts, and Gail was telling them all about her likes and loves as well as those things she couldn't stand. She handed them a paper. On it she'd written everything: Her favorite foods, her least favorite sport; her favorite and least favorite colors.

Richard thanked her and handed the paper over to Virginia. Birds twittered in the trees and the grass smelled of new growth. Spring was almost here.

***

Virginia finished the last of the pink cupcakes and shelved them behind the case. It was amazing, how the flavor (a rich strawberry) had taken over almost every sale at *Just Desserts*. The classes long ended, she and Richard were preparing for the little one. The crib was finally in the lavender room; though much of the room itself hadn't changed. Still, the baby's outfits of pink, yellow and purple peeked from inside the shelving, and whispers of 'little girl' surrounded the room in the form of pillows, play things and tiny polka dots.

It was Saturday, just three weeks before Gail's due date and everything was ready. She was ready. It felt as if she was pregnant and would soon deliver. She breathed in the pink frosting and slid the glass shut.

From behind her, Richard was getting the sweet rolls out of the oven and displaying them on cooling racks. It was morning, near 7 a.m., and only a few shoppers were walking, shopping and visiting. She hadn't seen God for nearly two months, but somehow her visits with him through prayer and scripture study had fed her mind and heart. She knew he was there even if she couldn't see him.

Richard was looking good. He'd started a diet plan just six weeks ago, and she could already see some changes, mostly around his middle. He smiled at her now and placed the pan on the cooling rack.

"You're deep in thought," he said.

"It's too perfect," she said. "I can hardly believe we're going to have a baby."

"And you look so good," he said.

She smiled down at her stomach. "Almost as nice as yours."

"So, you think I'm getting buff?"

"Something like that."

He held her close. "Can't look chubby for that new baby."

She laughed. "She'll be chubby for you."

"But that's different. So, what are we going to name her?"

They'd discussed multiple names but none had really spoken to her until she'd brought up the name, Joy.

"I still think, Joy," she said.

"But that's that little orphan girl's name."

"She has a mother."

"Right, but I don't know. Shouldn't we pick something inspiring?" he asked.

"Joy is inspiring. Her mother is inspiring. I'm grateful for both of them. Maybe...we can give this little girl a better life than either of them have likely had."

Richard smiled down at her. His eyes were warm. "Hmmm, I'll have to think about that."

***

A week later, Virginia wasn't feeling well, so Richard went to work without her. She spent the day in bed and nursed her flu with fluids and lots of television. By afternoon she was bored so she pulled out her Bible and began to read.

She'd discovered the verse that Richard had found a few months ago, and thought of it again as she pondered God's words: "And they said, Go to. Let us build us a city and a tower, whose top may reach into heaven... (Genesis 11:4)."

Was she reaching heaven?

Doing all of the right things was an interesting thought, but Virginia knew that it was much more about repentance than it was about being perfect. Life with God was about giving herself over to him; it was seeing his will for her more than the desires she had for herself. It was about trusting him; he would help her get into heaven.

She placed the stones before her like a map. One led to another until she reached the stone of constancy that led to the pink cupcake, commitment. Yes, she even had a pink cupcake with a ring in it. Tears welled then, though she wasn't sure why, but she was happy for the new commitment she'd made with Richard as well as with God. She was glad that they were a part of her life.

Reaching for the cupcake, she pulled out the ring. It glittered, though not gold. But it didn't have to be gold, it could be anything now, anything that drew her closer to God. Placing the ring on the coffee table she reached for the pink wrapping, and slowly pulled the pink paper away. Once off, she sat the wrinkled mess next to the ring and took a bite of cake.

It was yummy. The taste of strawberry melted and filled her mouth. With another bite came even more taste, and so she continued to bite and chew and swallow until the cupcake was finished and she could lick her fingers.

Boy, she made a heavenly cupcake!

When the phone rang moments later, she didn't hear it at first. Enjoying the last taste of strawberry leaving her lips, she finally stood and walked to the kitchen where her cell phone was sitting. It was Richard.

"Hello, lover!" she answered.

But he didn't reply.

"How are you feeling?" he finally managed.

"Much better. I just ate a cupcake."

"Well, you'll want to get over here as quickly as you can. There's been an accident."

"What? Where?"

"Now I don't want you to worry. I don't..."

"What is it?"

"It's Gail."

"What about Gail. Is she alright?"

"She's had the baby."

"The baby?"

"She's had the baby." Richard sounded so sad. She couldn't imagine what was wrong.

"Get to the hospital as soon as you can."

"What's wrong? What's wrong with the baby?"

"Do you want me to come and get you?"

"You mean you're already there?"

"They called. You were sick, but now..."

"What?"

"Virginia. Calm down. I'll come and get you."

"No, no." Virginia took a deep breath. Something was wrong with the baby but she had to get there. "I'll do it," she said, and then hung up before saying good-bye.

Racing into the baby's room she gathered her favorite little outfit, some booties, a blanket and a bottle. What else, what else? Yes, she remembered now. Everything else was packed in the diaper bag. She picked it up, stuffed the little things she'd gathered inside, and slung the bag over her shoulder.

***

She'd forgotten her jacket and it was cold. As the doors swung open, Virginia raced inside. She ran to the first booth she could see someone standing behind. She didn't look at the sign above or the people sitting near her. All she could think about was the baby.

"Labor and delivery!" she yelled.

A nurse stood, looked toward Virginia's feet, and then back at Virginia. "You don't..."

"It's not me, I'm...I'm the adoptive mother. I need to get to my baby!"

"Your name, please."

"Ah...Virginia. Virginia Bean I mean Virginia Green."

The woman looked down.

"Hurry, hurry!"

"The wife of Richard Green?"

"That's me!"

"Follow me."

Virginia followed behind the well-endowed woman. She walked slowly, and her legs were too short like a child's. Virginia was breathing heavy, she knew, but she also knew she needed to get to her husband and to her new baby. What was wrong? Why had Richard sounded so quiet? Was something wrong with the mother? She'd never considered that. Was something wrong with Gail? And all she could think about was the baby! *Please forgive me, Father!* she prayed. *And bless me, that no matter what happens that I will remember Thy great love for me. Thy will be done.*

At the end of her prayer they'd reached a room. She could see Richard inside and Gail lying on a bed, and she could see Gail's parents; she'd met them only once, when Gail had invited them to dinner at their home. But now they all looked solemn. It took all she had within her to walk inside.

Gail was crying, and so were her parents. Richard reached for her. The little baby carrier on wheels was empty.

***

Baby Joy was dead.

Gail had fallen down the stairs at her parent's home and they had raced her here, but not in time. The baby was gone.

"My baby!" Gail screamed, and in that instant Virginia wondered if the baby had ever been hers. Virginia took the petite girl in her arms and held her close. Gail shook and the cold returned to Virginia's arms. "I killed her, I killed my...baby."

Fresh tears creased Virginia's cheeks. She held the girl as she sobbed but the words wouldn't come. And then she felt a hand. She didn't turn but she knew instinctively that it wasn't Richard's. Still, the warmth that filled her was immeasurable.

"Do you forgive me?" the young girl asked.

As she felt the hand burn love within her there was only one thing she could say. "Yes, yes, I forgive you. It was an accident, a terrible accident."

The girl sobbed again, holding Virginia close.

Virginia heard Richard's voice. This time she turned to see him standing by the window. "Are you alright?"

She left Gail and raced to him. The top of his shirt was already wet and he cried along with her as even more tears came to his eyes. "I'm so sorry, Virginia, so sorry."

She felt so weary.

"How long have you been here?" she asked. She looked up then to see Gail's parents standing at either side of their daughter's bed.

"About two hours. I didn't want to worry you...until I knew."

"So where..."

"Do you want to see her? She's beautiful, just like we always wanted." He touched her face, and wiped away the tears.

"How is Gail?"

"She'll be alright. She's young and strong. So, do you want to see the baby?"

***

She was surprised at how peaceful she looked. How still. But she was gone. There was no light and the 7 lb 2 oz little girl was perfect.

***

"How are you doing?"

He was worried about her, although she'd told him otherwise. "I'm at peace," she said, holding him and crying. "It's God's will, and I will be alright."

He'd watched her in forthcoming weeks, when the due date arrived and the nursery remained empty. He'd watched her rock in the rocker in the baby's room. He'd watch as she handled the itty bitty clothes. He'd watched as she read her favorite children's books aloud in the lavender room. And he'd watch her as she cried.

But she didn't throw anything out. Not the crib, not the blankets, not the books. And after three weeks she was joining him again at work.

She looked pale, and she wasn't eating like he was used to seeing, but she was smiling and talking about starting up some new marriage classes. "Now, we have an even deeper element to share about children," she'd say. "Now that we have experienced it for ourselves."

And he would nod and hug her and pretend that he was doing as well as she was. "If it wasn't for him..."

When the day drew closer for their anniversary, he'd explained about the trip up the hill. It would be a remembrance of sorts, for their wedding day, now six years past. When she'd remained quiet and thoughtful, he'd put the matter aside for another day.

And now it was here.

***

The walk wasn't an easy one. In early spring the hill a few miles behind their Idaho cabin was as covered with snow as icing on one of her favorite cupcakes. She thought of the cupcake now, pink and ready.

Her boots stepped through the thick snow. The air was crisp and as Richard held her gloved hand, she thought of the last time they'd traversed this area. She couldn't help it. All the feelings came back, though this time the wilderness was covered in snow.

"So, where are we going?" she asked.

"My surprise," he said. But the way he said it, she knew.

The walk was a good 30 minutes on a summer day, and Richard was silent as she followed him from behind. They'd brought along plenty of water, some mixed nuts and dried fruit, and a couple of green apples – his favorite.

Her breath was floating through the air like ice skaters on wings. The trees were covered in white powder, and the top of the hill, that almost resembled a mountain, stood before them like a tower – her tower. How well she knew the changes that would need to be made. How well she knew where she had been and what it would mean to move forward, not only on this snow-covered trail, but in her life.

***

Richard's thoughts couldn't be restrained. He tried to remember the ceremony like it was yesterday...

"And do you, Richard, take Virginia as your lawfully wedded wife, to have and to hold, from this day forward, as long as you both shall live?"

"I do."

The eyes of the preacher had turned then to his future wife. She was resplendent in white satin and pearls; her blond hair was drawn up in wildflowers, unexpected strands of hair curled around her face. She wore no veil, and her smile took him in and carried him away.

"And do you, Virginia, take this man to be your lawfully wedded husband, to have and to hold, from this day forward, as long as you both shall live?"

There was a pause, and for a brief moment Richard wondered if she had changed her mind. And then he'd looked deeply into her eyes. Warmth was there, and love. "Yes," she'd said, although the appropriate words were to be, 'I do.' She looked at him, warmth filling her face, the feel of her hands in his connecting them both. And now?

As he held her hand, they walked. The snow was deep, and his love for her had increased. Six years later he loved her more than he could express.

"We're almost there," he breathed, a small fog coming from his mouth and filling the sky. "Are you ready?"

"For what?"

He thought again of the day he'd kissed her, long and lingering, on this very hill – wildflowers and a few friends and loved ones as their only backdrop. It was all he could do to remain patient as they took the last few steps to the top. "To marry me again."

***

She wasn't sure how he had done it, but the table was spread, a small table with lit candles and her best dishes. She would have killed him if she hadn't been so touched. And then there was the red heart tablecloth made of material, not one of those plastic kinds that you can find at the local dollar store. But that's not all. Somehow, he'd managed some violinists. They must have been shaking in their boots. They were playing music, what was it? She didn't know, but the soothing tune just made her cry. He took her hand.

"You know the first time we were here..." He wasn't looking at her but off into the distance as if reflecting on the first time. "...there were friends, some food, but not nearly the privacy afforded us now."

She blinked over at the violinists. The tone was slow in movement, almost like the day air that curled around her face.

"Except for them," she said.

He walked her to the table. "I think you should know that I've made some very fine plans, and not all of them have to do with food."

She giggled and sat down. There was nothing on the table other than the linens and dishes. She wondered what they were going to eat. Snow? The thought of it made her even more cold.

And then, in the distance she heard it, sort of like her car's wiper blades, but louder. In moments she could hear the helicopter as it reached the hill's peek. A metal bird, its blades whirred until the beast landed, the tablecloth fluttering slightly at its approach. The whirring continued and then slowed and stopped.

In seconds someone was getting out. Actually, there were two of them, including a boy who looked like the boy she'd seen that day stocking shelves at Wholesale Max's. The women who came out were familiar too. How had he roped *them* into this?

It was two of the ladies from her class! The young woman named Brianne and the middle-aged woman named Tracy whose husband had a huge thing for sports. They were carrying huge plastic tubs, walking through the snow like the troupers she had no idea they were. As they approached they opened the tubs. A sweet and memorable scent entered Virginia's nostrils. Why it smelled just like turkey with all of the trimmings!

"You're right, of course," said her husband as if he'd heard her. "We are having Thanksgiving early this year."

Virginia sat stunned as the women dished them up. Both were wearing red heart aprons over their coats. As expected they wore boots as well and handed them some hand warmers – something they'd forgotten to pack in Richard's eagerness to get up the hill.

"Now, you're going to have to eat sort of fast," Tracy said. "It's sort of like the Winter Olympics up here, though I know it's spring down there. The helicopter pilot assures me that he will be back for you in a short time to take you down."

Richard smiled over at her and then looked down at his steaming plate of turkey, potatoes, yams, rolls and pumpkin pie. "I'll have you know," he said clearly for all to hear, "that this is by far the coldest Thanksgiving meal I've ever experienced."

"We'll leave you then," said Brianne, waving to the other woman. They took the containers and walked to the helicopter. The violinists were still playing. It was as soothing, but the cold was feeling its way through her pores. The downdraft from the helicopter blades rushed near them again and in a few moments the helicopter lifted into the sky and was gone.

Richard smiled. "Now, they'll be back in about 20 minutes or so. By that time we should be halfway through with our meal and I can do what I came here to do."

"Surely, not *that*..." Virginia said, taking a bite of potatoes.

"No, *that* is reserved for later. The *extra dessert* if you will."

Virginia giggled, she couldn't help it. Fortunately, the chairs were padded with a red cushion. She couldn't imagine sitting on frigid wood. Still, the seat was not heated. She'd already placed the warmers down her boots and those in her hands were heating up nicely.

A few minutes into the meal Richard stood, motioned to the violinists, and dropped next to her on one knee. She could imagine the chill quickly traveling up his leg as it met the snow. The song was their wedding song, and all Virginia could think about was the glorious warmth and happiness of that day. It was cold, but not as cold as today. Spring had come much earlier that year and Virginia could still smell the new buds peeking out from green in some places and from snow in others.

Richard reached inside his coat pocket and pulled out a ring. At first, she imagined it as one of those nasty ones, the old cheap things she used in the cupcakes, but then...

"Now, I know exactly what you're thinking," he said, "but I want you to know I had it sized perfectly for your *right* hand."

"My right hand?" Virginia turned from the sweet smell that was quickly growing cold.

"Hold it out."

Virginia put down her fork and held out her hand. "If you will remove the glove, please." He grinned mischievously up at her.

Against her better judgment, but captivated by his smile, Virginia removed the glove along with the hand warmer. He slid the ring on. It was warm and it was real.

"Why..."

"Now I want you to know that I spent a lot of money on this," Richard said, surprising her more. "But that's not why I bought it."

"Okay?"

"Well, it spoke to me. It said, 'This is the ring for your wife. She needs to know how much you love her. She needs to know that the baby will come.'"

"It really said that?" Hearing the voice of God was one thing, but hearing the voice of a ring? Okay, so it was like hearing a voice from the stones. She could believe anything.

"You'd better switch knees. This one's going to freeze off."

"Not until you tell me you'll marry me again "

"Sure. Now get off that knee."

He switched knees.

"Now that you've said yes, I'd like a kiss." He pursed his lips.

She leaned over, her Thanksgiving meal in May forgotten. The kiss was long and sweet and reminded her of the one shared just a few short years ago.

"I want you to remember this cold day with the lovely Thanksgiving meal, and I want you to remember how much I love you."

"I love you, too," she squeaked, for suddenly the cold was gone and all she could think about was how much she loved him. And something else. She'd waited and waited and waited for the right moment, and of all things, her sweet husband had given it to her.

"Thank you for the beautiful ring," she said, "but I'm getting cold."

***

Virginia pulled off the glove and fingered the ring on her right hand. "You're a pretty strange man," she said. "Why didn't you have the helicopter pick us up in the first place?"

"And miss the great hike? I don't think so." He laughed.

He turned from the helicopter window. Fresh tears were falling down his cheeks. "This ring's our new commitment, to each other and to God."

"I love it. But what about my commitment to you. I don't have a ring for you."

"You don't need one."

"But I do."

"Just count the ring I gave you as a commitment for us both."

"But it doesn't work that way. When we land, let's go shopping for a new ring. I have something to tell you anyway."

His eyebrows raised. The helicopter was landing. It appeared to be stopping at some helicopter port near a mansion.

"The boy and his father," he answered.

She could barely see the top of the boy's head from where she was sitting, but there was definitely two of them sitting up front.

Richard reached for her hand. The metal blades whirred to a stop and the man and his son got out.

Again, she noticed the striking resemblance to the boy that God had gone to help at Wholesale Max's.

The older man shook each of their hands and Richard thanked him for the free flight.

But it was the younger one who spoke.

"Hi," he said. "Have a good time?"

"We did." She couldn't help thinking of the day that God had left her standing alone in favor of going to the boy who stocked the shelves. The boy in front of her now appeared to be the same young man. Hadn't God called him Trevor? She had stood quite a distance from him then...still...

"How has your work been going at Wholesale Max's?" she decided to ask.

He seemed momentarily surprised. He looked at her closely for the first time and appeared to consider her words as well as her face.

And then a surprising thought struck Virginia. Could Trevor be the father of Gail's child?

"Good, much better, thank you," he said.

Trevor walked away with his father, and then quite unexpectedly he turned, allowing his father to walk ahead. Virginia's car was parked in front of the mammoth house, ready for their return to their humble abode, but something had struck the boy, and he was grasping for the right words.

She watched as the cool air brushed against his hair, the way he stood in that thoughtful position, hands to his side, his eyes looking slightly up. He shifted his feet.

A chord had definitely been struck.

"And you, are you feeling better since losing your baby?" he asked.

Her heart thundered in her chest. Her baby. He had called the baby, hers. "You know...Gail?" she asked.

He colored slightly. "I love her, you know. I want you to know that."

Virginia imagined God then, walking up to Trevor, the boy standing before her now, the same boy she'd been *put out* about at Wholesale Max's. She imagined him taking the chocolate cake to the boy and telling him something about cakes and how it's the frosting that takes the cake or something like that. She imagined him spilling the beans about commitment; and she imagined that the boy felt love and joy within his soul.

***

Their shopping finished, Virginia placed the newly purchased ring on the frosted pink cupcake and walked to the living room. It was the same routine every night. Leave your shoes on the floor by the bed and your clothing next to it. Put on pajamas. Go into the bathroom, take off rings. Wash face. Brush teeth. Go into the living room. Watch T.V.

As she watched the silver ring glitter on the top of the cupcake, Virginia thought about how much she loved Richard and how much she loved God. After everything they had been through, she had begun to really listen to God. Her trust in him consumed her. It really was about doing her best and trusting in God's will for her. And if she listened, she could do that, even if she didn't like it.

Optimism wasn't something she carried around simply for the sake of carrying it. She carried it always, whether her life was turning out the way she expected it to, or not. She just kept going. Kept going. Not on her own, but with God. Always with God. The constancy with God was a consistent walk, through thorns as well as roses.

Would it be tough?

She touched her belly. Like a glittering ring on a pink cupcake, surprises came when you least expected them. After continuing to feel sick for weeks, she'd decided to go in for a checkup. Her tiredness, her queasiness actually meant something. She laughed to herself as she remembered jumping off the examination table buck naked.

Would it continue to be tough?

Yes. But with God and Richard at her side, she knew she would make it.

Kathryn Elizabeth Jones

The Feast
A Spiritual Guide

The Ring

- Marriage means helping each other.
- Trials are necessary.
- Humility helps you to hear God.
- Miracles happen every day. They often come in small packages.
- Communication takes work and patience.
- Sometimes you have to try again.
- Sometimes you don't get what you want when you want it.
- When miracles happen, you don't always see them.
- Sometimes you get too comfortable with life.
- Sometimes you avoid the one you love instead of facing the problem head on.
- Sarcasm rarely helps an already tender situation.
- When God speaks peace to your heart, that's a message, too.

The Vow

- You cannot force your way into heaven.
- Pray even when you're angry. Especially when you're angry.
- You create the distance between you and God.
- Optimism has its boundaries – without God.
- Jealousy can creep in when you least expect it.
- God provides in mysterious ways.
- A gesture of service can open both windows and doors.
- Prayer opens the heart to hearing answers.
- God's will for you is not always the same as your will for yourself.

The Choice

- Yes, the timing of God is everything.
- Commitment travels three ways.
- Pay attention to life. It might just tell you something.
- Answers take work.
- Sometimes our spouse will surprise us for the better.
- An open mind does wonders for disappointment.
- God may speak to you unexpectedly, be ready to respond quickly.
- Again, jealousy creeps in when you least expect it.
- Forgiveness is key.

The Feast

- Waiting takes patience but it helps with understanding.
- Everything you go through in life lends instruction.
- Have faith.
- Repent.
- Forgive.
- Perfection comes in the next life.
- See God's will for you and have the courage to follow it.
- Learn through experience.
- Commitment to God is key to success.

Notes

Notes

Notes